Sara's Song

Tina Jones Williams

Sara's Song
Copyright 2016
Tina Jones Williams

Bibliographical Data:
Williams, Tina Jones
ISBN: 978-1523379330
General Fiction

Prelude:
"This is Always"
"Stolen Moments"

First Verse:
"In a Sentimental Mood"

Refrain:
"I Was Telling Her About You"
"I Could Have Told You"
"Good Morning Heartache"

Second Verse:
"Fine and Mellow"
"Come Dance With Me"

Chorus:
"Nature Boy"

Third Verse:
"Round Midnight"

Refrain:
"Every Time We Say Goodbye"
"Don't Go To Strangers"

Fourth Verse:
"Joy Comes In the Morning"
"I'll Be Seeing You"

Prelude:

"This Is Always"

Sara Jameson has been called many things in her lifetime; Colored, Negro and most recently Black. Sara ignores labels and other people's assessments, believing they often are attempts to define, confine or worst case endeavor to malign. Always dancing to her own tune Sara carefully crafts her song, setting the large and small moments of life to music.

Sara's song began in rural Arkansas where she and her small family lived quietly and harmoniously in rented quarters on a small farm. In 1933 prior to Sara starting high school they moved to a rambling high rise apartment building in a loud cacophonous city; Chicago. To her surprise and delight, Sara fell in love with Chicago. She grew fond of everything; especially the cadence of the South side where she lived, and Du Sable High where she discovered Jazz, the embodiment of her first real love; rhythm and flow.

4

In her senior year, a few blocks away from Du Sable she found another love, Ben Jameson. Fairly new to the city, unlike Sara, Ben did not love Chicago. But Ben loved Sara; she was tall and shapely with a butter cream complexion, soft pretty features and a quiet purposeful way. By comparison, Ben, prone to action, a few well chosen words, tall, dark with angular features and quite handsome, they made a pretty picture.

They stood shoulder to shoulder when Sara was in heels, but rarely did they see eye to eye. They married in 1938. By 1943 they were home owners living in Berkeley, California. Why they chose Berkeley is anyone's guess.

No doubt their story, when set to music, makes a seductive song.

"Stolen Moments"

From her usual vantage point on the sofa under the window in the living room of their home on Julia Street in Berkeley, Sara saw the mailman as he climbed the front stairs. She opened the door as he waved a large white envelope.

"I think this is what you've been waiting for" he said with a smile.

Returning his smile, taking the envelope and her other letters Sara replied "I think you're right, I'm a little afraid to open it."

"Don't be, the big envelope is the one you want," he replied with a wink.

"Well thanks for bringing me something other than bills today," said a distracted Sara.

Still talking as he headed down the stairs, the mailman's response was lost as Sara focused on the envelope in her hand. Closing the door, tearing the flap, Sara felt the quickening tempo and an excitement that was hers alone. This time she was excited for herself, for her own possibilities. She knew the possibilities were endless.

Smiling as she considered the contents of the envelope, Sara refilled her coffee cup, lit another cigarette, took her place on the sofa and without invitation events from her life played vividly as the boundaries of time and place disappeared.

First Verse:

"In a Sentimental Mood"

Outside the window it was pitch black; so dark the slight jostling of the train had been the only evidence they were still moving. The second of a three day trip traveling with her three young children; Tessa (also Sara's mother's name) was four, Ronald three, and Gregory a newborn; Sara was tired. Chatting quietly with the woman sitting across the aisle Sara had shared "Meeting you is a stroke of luck. Without you, I'm not sure how I would have managed."

"I'm glad to help. My children are at the age where they consider themselves 'independent' and I'm happy to let them be just that" replied Joan, Sara's new friend and traveling companion. Joan had been only too happy to take care of Sara's children whenever Sara needed a moment to herself. The two women had talked openly; perhaps it was the anonymity and the fact that Joan was moving to Southern California and they likely would never see each other again that had given them permission to speak freely.

All of the children had been sleeping as the train drew closer to Berkeley when Sara had whispered, "I'm sure this is just nerves but a small voice has asked 'what would you do if Ben isn't there to meet you at the station'? I don't know anyone else in Berkeley and I'm not even sure where our rooms are located. I know I'm being silly, like my mother always says 'don't borrow trouble.' Of course he'll be there."

And he was. When Sara saw Ben standing on the platform she had taken a deep breath, the first real breath she'd taken since leaving Chicago; reminding herself that she could count on Ben, she had to count on Ben.

For the two months prior to Sara's move, she and Ben had been living apart. Sara had stayed in Chicago tying up loose ends; sorting through their belongings to determine what should stay in their new life and what should be given away or tossed. She had closed out relationships, making sure that friends she wanted to maintain would be able to reach them in their new home. For his part, Ben had begun working as soon as he'd arrived in town, he had found an appropriate place for his family to live while their house was being built and had generally organized their new lives in Berkeley.

The decision to move had been more difficult for Sara than it had been for Ben. He had already left his family home when he made his move to Chicago. Relocating to Berkeley had required Sara to move away from her home and from the people she had loved all of her life. After considering all of the options, lots of discussions and prayer, Sara and Ben had concluded the best opportunities for their family, employment, education and housing, were in California. Their decision to move had mirrored the one made in the early 1940's by many Colored people in pursuit of a better life.

On the platform theirs had been a happy reunion. Almost at the same time Ben and Sara had whispered "You're here." Ben had gently touched Sara and each of the children as if to make sure they were just as he'd left them.

Ronald was the first to speak asking, "Is this California?"

Ben smiled as he replied, "In all its glory."

With a three year olds' confidence Ronald had declared, "I like it."

After securing their luggage, the family had made the short drive to the South Berkeley boarding house in silence as Sara and the children eagerly took in Berkeley, their new home. In addition to the vast visual differences, Sara had felt the change in rhythm, silently comparing Chicago to Berkeley. At that time of night on the Southside of Chicago the streets would have been alive with people, all looking for something to do. There were always places to go and people to see. In contrast the streets in Berkeley had seemed expansive and empty but not deserted or desolate; Sara had surmised people were happily nestled inside rather than out pursuing the next thing.

In those days Berkeley was a small town disguised as a city and it had worn its uniqueness with enthusiasm. By many, Berkeley would have only been described as ideal. The weather was mild, never too hot or too cold, it didn't snow and there were no floods, no tsunamis. The biggest complaint was about the fog which usually burned off by 10 or 11 am. Berkeley's crime rate was low and the population was stable. The University of California at Berkeley was able to attract top scholars, intellectuals and idealistic young people to add to the mix of an already eclectic population. Transportation into, around, and out of Berkeley had been made convenient by the trolley system, the San Francisco Bay Bridge, the Golden Gate Bridge and Southern Pacific Railroad. What was not to like?

Six weeks in rented rooms had gone by quickly. For two evenings before the move into their new home on Julia Street, Ben and Sara had packed their things into a borrowed truck. Their few belongings had fit easily; they had only their beds, a chair and desk, record player, records and radio, toiletries, linens and clothing. Most of those items either Ben had bought while he waited for them to arrive or Sara had shipped from Chicago. To fully furnish their new home they would need to purchase a few necessities immediately while adding "wants" over time. Sara, not a patient or inherently frugal shopper would need to rein in her desire to fill the empty spaces until they were better able to afford the things she wanted.

Taking a last look around the two rooms that had been their home for six weeks Sara had said to Ben, "I admit when the children and I got here I was shocked by the size of this house and a little apprehensive about sharing such close quarters with so many strangers, but I've been pleasantly surprised. In spite of the closeness, almost everybody minds their own business unless invited into a conversation. Of course, Leona is the exception," Sara had added with a smile, "The norm seems to be no personal questions asked and very little personal information is volunteered. Again, except in Leona's case."

Ben had laughed at Sara's comments about Leona, her first friend in Berkeley.

On the surface Sara and Leona were nothing alike but they had taken an instant liking to one another. Their differences were obvious; where Sara was tall, Leona was short, Sara's complexion was light Leona's was dark, and where Sara could be a bit cool Leona was always warm. Leona's smile could stop even the most discontent person mid rant.

When they first met Leona had taken Sara under her wing sharing her knowledge of the house and the city. Leona knew everything and everybody. Sara and Leona had developed a close friendship that proved invaluable to Sara and was enjoyable for Leona. After several days when Sara had mentioned that maybe she would look for a job, Leona had encouraged Sara to join her and the others from the house who worked on the swing shift at the Richmond Shipyards. At that time the United States was embroiled in a dual war, fighting fascism abroad and racism at home. Most of the residents of Mrs. Knight's house worked at the Richmond Shipyards in support of the war effort as did most of the Colored wage earners living in Berkeley. Leona had often quipped "It took a world war to get us out of White folks' kitchens." To seal the deal, Leona had shared that Mrs. Knight, the owner of the house, a kind middle aged Colored woman, provided care for the children while their parents were working and hot meals for a small increase in the rent. As the only kitchen in the house was located on the first floor where Mrs. Knight lived, these arrangements had worked out well for the residents.

Sara had been hired on the spot as a welder on the swing shift and started the same day. After filling out her paperwork she was issued a uniform that consisted of a long sleeved shirt worn buttoned up to the neck and long pants, both made of natural fibers, steel toed boots, a full face helmet with flip-up visor and heavy duty leather gloves. Her tasks were simple and her training was brief and effective.

After a few nights on the job while relaxing in Mrs. Knight's warm welcoming kitchen, Sara had felt comfortable enough to share her perceptions of working at the Shipyards with Leona and Mrs. Knight.

"Some of our male coworkers are offended by the fact that I am a woman, add to that I'm a Colored woman and it's almost too much for them to bear. They are not shy about voicing their displeasure; their meanness is so constant it's almost background noise."

Mrs. Knight responded with a knowing smile as she shook her head. She knew only too well the kinds of comments that Sara was talking about. She also recognized the mask that Sara wore while describing the comments because she wore one herself. She knew first hand it took considerable effort to appear unfazed while you were hurt inside.

Sara had continued, "No matter how badly we're treated at work we have a much easier time than many of our coworkers. We have a roof over our heads thanks to you and a bed to call our own. So many people came to town with no place to stay and only enough money to make the trip. They may have gotten a job but they had nowhere to live and nobody to ask for help."

Sara and her coworkers had been working on the most efficiently built U. S. war ships being launched at the time. At the height of the United States' involvement in the war, 98,000 former farmers, share croppers and laborers had converged on Richmond, California at the request of the Government to abandon non-war related employment. Workers were invited in mass to the shipyards to build ships faster than any war ships had ever been built before. Start to finish, some ships were built and launched in a total of three and a half days. The shipyards were in operation three shifts, twenty four hours per day, seven days a week.

Before the war, Richmond just eight miles from Berkeley was a small homogenous town of 23,000 prior to the arrival of the diverse group of almost 100,000 workers who were all races, backgrounds, and cultures. They had brought with them cultural differences, language barriers, varied expectations and deeply rooted prejudices.

The city had not been equipped to handle so many new comers; housing, childcare, and transportation for the workers proved to be huge problems. Near the shipyards for convenience some housing units for White shipyard managers were hastily built. Two types of housing were constructed; small cottages for senior level managers and multiple unit apartment buildings for lower level managers. Everyone else had to fend for himself. Due to lack of housing a large number of shipyard workers had slept in cars, pick-up trucks and some in train boxcars forming a small boxcar village. Many workers lived outside of Richmond in the surrounding towns of Berkeley, Oakland and San Francisco. Transportation needs had been met by the Key System Rails, which had quickly laid new tracks linking Berkeley and Oakland to the Shipyards. Workers living across the San Francisco Bay traveled to work by ferry.

Shipyard-subsidized childcare facilities were opened a few miles away, where children of management were placed first and any remaining openings had been given to the children of White workers. Everyone else had to fend for themselves.

Once Sara had become acclimated to the work environment, the welder job had not been difficult to learn. She was grateful for the pay if not for the uniform and the repetitive nature of the job. It's no telling how long she would have stayed at the Shipyards but the decision to leave came quickly and without question. When she had arrived home at her usual time wearing her spare clothing rather than her uniform, she had explained to Ben, "I was fairly resigned to the job until tonight; in spite of all of the protective gear I was wearing, a stray spark landed in my hair and caught fire, I guess a strand came loose from my braid. I smelled my hair burning before I saw it.

Fortunately we keep a water bottle at our side for just this reason. I furiously sprayed my hair and after I was certain the fire was out, I informed my supervisor tonight would be my last." The timing of Sara's hair accident had fit with their planned move. Sara and Ben had agreed the decision for her to quit eliminated the need for childcare and the associated logistical problems.

On the day of their move to the new house, all morning, although still very early, other residents had stopped by to wish the Jamesons well in their new home and to remind them that they too would be moving on. As Ben, Sara and the children got into the truck to leave the boarding house for the last time, a small group had gathered including Leona and Mrs. Knight. Sara and Leona had vowed to stay in touch though Sara thought it was unlikely.

Approaching the truck Mrs. Knight had said simply, "May the Lord bless you and keep you," as she and the others waved their goodbyes, sending the Jamesons on their way.

Touched by their kindness, Sara had tucked all of the memories away for another day.

They made the short drive from the boarding house to their new home in less than fifteen minutes while Ronald, as usual, was full of questions and Tessa listened quietly while taking in the sights.

Riding through Berkeley, Ronald asked, "Will there be kids on our new street?"

Ben answered warmly, "There are plenty of kids living on Julia Street."

Ronald followed up with, "Is there a park?"

"There are two parks within walking distance, San Pablo Park and Grove Street Park," replied Sara.

"Will they like us?" Tessa asked anxiously.

"I'm sure they will," Sara replied with her usual confidence.

When looking back Sara had always considered the train ride cross country and the stay in the boarding house as sort of a prelude, with the move into their new home the main event. She recalled that morning, as they pulled into their driveway on Julia Street she'd noticed another family moving in further down the block and had looked forward to meeting them along with the rest of her new neighbors.

Once inside, the whole family had concentrated on getting settled and by mid-day the Jamesons had moved in their belongings without incident. Their new home did not disappoint. It was brand new and had generous proportions by 1940's standards; a large living room, connecting dining room and two bedrooms. Standing in the middle of the living room Sara had confided to no one in particular "I never imagined owning a home; the notion was foreign to me. Having grown up in rented space on a small farm and then in apartments shared with my parents and adult relatives, home ownership always seemed like a fantasy. I admit I have never spent much time on daydreams." On this occasion Sara had made an exception. She imagined the good times that lay ahead as she circled her cozy new living room. She held Gregory with one arm and gestured with the other, commenting, "I can see our Christmas tree in that corner over between those two windows, framed by drapes in a shade of emerald green, my favorite color." The others had stared in the direction she indicated as if they shared her vision.

As she continued her imaginary tour Sara recalled that Ben had always been sure that one day he would own a home; he had known he would either buy it or build it himself and he had the carpentry skills to back up that promise. His sense of certainty was one of the qualities Sara had admired about him; he seemed to have no doubt when it came to his plans for their future. Their new home was a testament to Ben's surefooted approach to getting things done. He had said it could be done and they had done it.

She had walked around their modest home, running her fingers along the cabinetry and the countertops admiring them as if she had never seen anything more beautiful. Sara had exclaimed, "It's really lovely! Look at the hardwood floors, they're beautiful. When our new sofa arrives next week we can put it here under the window or over there on that long wall." Tessa and Ronald had trailed behind Sara, seemingly delighted by their new home, moving from one room into the next, surveying the details and no doubt imagining the life they would build.

In the kitchen, Sara said as she had examined the appliances, "They're brand new, they are exactly what I would have chosen and the fixtures are so shiny they sparkle." Ben had watched with satisfaction; being a carpenter he was pleased with the quality of the workmanship and he was pleased with Sara's reaction. He was happy that his wife was happy.

Julia Street was only two blocks long, 1500 and 1600. The 1500 block, their block, bordered by Sacramento Street a major thoroughfare on one end and California Street a sleepy two lane road on the other. That day, the whole neighborhood showed to its best advantage; flowers were in bloom, trees were still in full blossom. Sidewalks had been swept, lawns mowed, yards beautifully appointed.

In spite of the chores remaining to be tackled indoors, the neighbors already in residence had surrendered to the pull of the unknown and had taken advantage of the opportunity to meet the new families moving onto their street. A group of women had assembled at the end of the block waiting for a glimpse of the new families. They might have been anxious and excited to meet their new neighbors, surely hoping they would become new friends.

Squaring her shoulders Sara had said to Ben, "I guess I better get this done sooner rather than later," feeling nervous and hopeful that their new neighborhood would live up to all of their expectations and dreams. Ben had glanced over and nodded as she, with Gregory perched on her hip, ventured outdoors. At the same moment the other new neighbor appeared out front with a young girl at her side. Both women dressed casually for a major move, had stepped out and walked tentatively down the sidewalk toward the circle of waiting women.

Admiring the surroundings, smelling the freshly cut grass and the fragrance of the flowers, they had stopped just short of the group where Sara and her new neighbor faced each other.

Sara had extended her hand, smiling as she said, "Hi, I'm Sara Jameson and this is Gregory."

Grasping Sara's hand, the woman had replied "Hello, I'm Mary Grabel and this is our daughter Jeannette."

While Sara and Mary had exchanged happy greetings, Sara's other children appeared at her side demanding attention and introductions. A quick review of their children's names and ages were exchanged as the children ran off to join the other youngsters waiting impatiently further down the block.

As Mary cooed quietly to Gregory, she and Sara fell into an easy conversation including the due date of the much anticipated arrival within a few weeks of Mary's second child. They had quickly shared detailed information about their husbands and plans for their new homes. Their plans were extensive and most likely expensive, including the anticipated day-care needs for the children and many of the other things they had in common. They had eagerly agreed to meet later in the week for a cup of coffee and to fill in more blanks after the move was complete. Although their conversation had been brief, a bond and an alliance had been formed between the two women. Sara Jameson and Mary Grabel, new found friends, had continued down the block together to meet their new neighbors.

The Julia Street women had been out in full force. When Mary and Sara approached the group, a smiling woman had reached for Gregory asking, "May I," carefully taking him from Sara and securely holding him away from the grasp of other eager arms. As an indulgent

Gregory, with his dimpled cheeks and curly dark brown hair, was passed from one pair of waiting arms into another, Sara had briefly shared the story of her three-day train ride from Chicago to Berkeley.

"My husband Ben, who is inside putting the children's beds together, came to California during the summer to find work and complete the purchase of our home. Once the details were in order I took the train from Chicago with our two older children, Tessa and Ronald and this one, our youngest, Gregory. We arrived here just a month-and-a-half ago, staying in temporary housing until our home was ready. While it was all an adventure, it is not an adventure I hope to repeat."

Everyone had made sympathetic sounds about Sara's journey as another woman introduced herself as Mrs. Simpson to the new-comers. She had then shared that her home was a few doors down from Sara's; it was clearly the most meticulous home in the neighborhood. She was a very light complexioned older woman with silver hair that hung attractively down her back. She was impeccably groomed and dressed to perfection in a twin sweater set made of cashmere and a matching wool skirt, perfect for a planned outing on a crisp fall day. Her accessories, an oblong silk scarf of subdued fall colors, worn with gold earrings and a bangle, were understated and completely appropriate for the outfit and the woman wearing them.

Inclining her head toward Sara and Mary, she said, "Hello, I'm Mrs. Simpson. My husband, Mr. Simpson and I are the only original owners left on this block. We have lived here for a number of years and have watched homes being built and neighbors come and go. "Welcome," she said while pointing out her pristine front yard. "As you can see we care about our neighborhood and we are fastidious about keeping our yards, our homes and our cars up to par and I'm sure your families will do the same."

Turning her head toward Sara and Mary's children and glancing at Mary's very pregnant physique, she had exclaimed, "Oh my, are those your children? So many already and you're both so young. Surely you are not planning to have more."

With that comment, the group of women fell silent, allowing Sara time to recall having heard Mrs. Simpson's voice before. It wasn't so much her voice that had stayed with Sara, as her manner, dripping with condescension. Sara remembered the prior week when she had come to the new house to take measurements for their new sofa, their one splurge. She had found the front door of her home standing open as a workman inside was finishing the final details. Sara had continued inside, began hurriedly taking the needed measurements, when she heard a voice coming from the only bathroom.

"Certainly not the highest quality materials, are they?" There was no answering voice.

Armed with the information she came for, Sara had chosen not to stay and meet the person who had made such an unkind and cutting remark. Meeting Mrs. Simpson, Sara was able to place the person with the voice. The silence had allowed her recollections to linger until interrupted by a woman with a most welcoming smile who had stepped forward introducing herself as Eva Parker. Sara liked her immediately.

Eva, like the other women on Julia Street, had dressed with obvious care. Her makeup and hairstyle, though understated, were quite becoming and her clothes seemed tailor-made. Sara was not surprised when one of the women mentioned that Eva was her hairdresser. Eva's outfit, a simple pair of maroon and black-plaid capri pants with a coordinating maroon sweater, and her manner, were more casual and more in keeping with a Saturday afternoon. She and the other women had been far more kind and welcoming than the formidable Mrs. Simpson. Eva had been quick to put Sara at ease by sharing, "I am delighted to live next door to your family, including the children." She had also stated warmly acknowledging Mary's advanced stage of pregnancy, "My husband and I don't have children, but we enjoy them." Sara had known at that moment that she and Eva would be friends.

Mrs. Simpson had made no reply to Eva's comments as she had begun walking in the direction of her home, adding over her shoulder, "It was nice to have made your acquaintance. I'm sure I'll have occasion to see you both in the neighborhood." As she continued toward her home she added, "I am willing to make recommendations on what to do with your yards."

Once out of earshot, the other women, after introducing themselves to Mary and Sara, gave their unvarnished opinions of Mrs. Simpson. Having felt a bit overwhelmed by the whole experience, Sara hadn't been able to keep track of all of the women's names, but their comments had resonated with her. Eva, whose name she did remember, said, "Mrs. Simpson doesn't have any children and doesn't really like children. She especially doesn't like any child who wanders into her yard."

Another woman added, "She seems to dislike almost anyone from the neighborhood who ventures uninvited into her yard."

A third neighbor had shared with the group, "She has a very high opinion of herself and the hand full of others who own the more expensive homes on this block. Mr. and Mrs. Simpson tend to spend their free time with them. One of her favorite sayings," the same neighbor added in an exaggerated imitation of Mrs. Simpson's voice, "'Dear, they may be our color but that doesn't make them our kind.'"

Someone else had added a bit sheepishly breaking the tension, "But she does dress well."

They had all chuckled.

Mrs. Simpson aside, the women were quite lovely. The spirited conversation revealed almost all of the women had a husband, children, a job and possessed a warm and welcoming personality. It had also been clear those remaining in the circle did not share Mrs. Simpson's openly broadcast beliefs about the superiority of Colored people who had lighter skin tones or so-called prestigious jobs. Sara placed no value on the "caste system" among Colored people and was pleased to find that most of her new neighbors dismissed those notions as well.

As the conversation had wound down and chores beckoned, Eva, leaving the group, had said laughingly with a smile, "Great to have met you. Welcome to the neighborhood. Both of you feel free to have as many children as you like." Everyone laughed.

Then Millicent, who had joined the group late wearing an outfit not at all like the others', an off the shoulder sweater, very tight skirt and very high heeled mules, had stood outside of the circle sipping what appeared to be a cocktail, offered dismissively as she walked away "Or as many as you can afford." No one laughed.

Later, on their first night, tucked in their new home after everyone had gone to bed, Sara picked up her old habit of sitting quietly in the dark with a cup of cold coffee and a cigarette while singing along softly to her favorite records. As their new sofa had not yet arrived she had dragged a chair next to the window in the living room where the sofa would sit. Sara had felt melancholy; she missed her family in Chicago. She had especially missed her mother and of course, her father.

Sara loved her father, but in a passive sort of way. She had spoken to him fairly regularly via telephone, recounting the news from her end and eagerly listening to any updates that he had to share. He had not "affiliated" with anyone after he and Sara's mother had separated and as best as Sara could tell, he lived a rather solitary life. He had moved away from Chicago, where he had lived with his brother, Ted, and Ted's wife. Sara had spent many hours listening as her father shared his experiences of when he first moved to Detroit. He painted a vivid picture of droves of people from the South arriving in Detroit in hopes of landing a job building "fighting" equipment in support of the war. Their mass arrival had overwhelmed the city. People were living "way too many" for the space. They were sleeping in shifts on the floor, in closets, on porches and in cars. There were long lines of people waiting everywhere: lines for information, lines for food, lines for housing and even longer lines for transportation. His stories had reminded Sara of how things were in Richmond, California at the height of employment at the Shipyards.

More than anything or anyone, Sara missed her mother; Sara had an "all in" relationship with her. She treasured her mother. Mrs. Crawford was the yardstick by which Sara measured all women, including Sara herself. She thought fondly of her and the traits that made her so special, including her mother's habit of quietly whispering, "thank you Jesus" whenever she sat down, leaving Sara to wonder again, whether her mother was thankful for the opportunity to sit or for having a place to sit. Whatever the motivation, Sara had been increasingly charmed by her mother's expressions of gratitude. In Sara's biased opinion, she was the most selfless, kind, wise, gentle, compassionate, talented woman she had ever known or was likely to meet. She appreciated all her mother had done for her and her family. Theirs was a love that was all encompassing and no doubt a joy to witness.

While still thinking of her family so far away, Sara had gone to bed.

The next morning, bright and early, Sara had said to Ben, "Before the neighbors begin leaving for church, I'd like to take a walk around our new neighborhood. I'm excited to see everything on my own."

Walking down the front steps, turning left at the end of the walkway, passing Mrs. Simpson's yard, Sara had noticed though the yard was beautiful it had a spiked fence around the perimeter which likely encouraged passersby to stay away. In contrast just next door, inviting a closer look was a completely accessible yard featuring an oversized picture window at the front of Mrs. McArthur's home. Moving to the lawn's edge, Sara had admired the gorgeous hats on display above the discreet milliner sign in the large window. Encouraged by the display, Sara had allowed herself another brief day dream where she wondered about the women who purchased the hats and where they might wear them.

Sara walked back in the opposite direction, approached the sidewalk on Sacramento Street and turned her attention to the array of businesses. Sara took inventory of the well-kept store fronts. On the furthest side of the street was a gas station, two grocery stores, a pharmacy, a variety store, a liquor store, a tiny night club, pool hall, a small post office, a doctor's office and a beauty shop. On the other side of Sacramento was another liquor store, a restaurant, a jewelry store, a creamery and another gas station. These businesses, like most of the homes in the neighborhood, were owned by Colored people. Most notable was Rumford's Pharmacy owned by Byron Rumford, who Sara later discovered, was the first colored pharmacist in Berkeley.

Mr. Rumford would some years later become the first Black Assemblyman from Northern California. While in office he would author the Fair Housing Legislation changing the face of home ownership. Sara was convinced that having so many successful businesses at arm's length would prove to be a major convenience and a source of pride to share with her children in the future as they decided which paths to follow and dreams to pursue.

It had all felt familiar. She was reminded of Chicago.

When it was time to head back, Sara noticed families wearing their Sunday best clearly on their way to church. Many of her new neighbors had smiled and waved and she had returned their friendly greetings. She had stepped onto the median to cross Sacramento Street, carefully sidestepping the embedded train tracks shared by the Santa Fe and Southern Pacific Railroads. Sara was told trains ran several times a day and she had remembered hearing the whistle at least once in the wee hours of the morning. She had wondered if their new home was on the right side of the tracks.

Back home, under Ben's supervision her family had been putting things away, finding a place for most everything, and creating order in place of the chaos resulting from the move. It was moments like this one that reminded Sara of why she had been drawn to Ben in the first place. He was quietly competent and handled things without fanfare or too much ado. He simply got things done, a skill that Sara wished she possessed and one she admired.

While she fed Gregory, Sara shared the details of her short walk, "This street has such an interesting mix of homes; each has its own personality which in some cases seems to match the owner's. Mrs. Simpson's home is quite lovely but a bit off-putting, but right next door the

McArthur home is open and charming, just like Mrs. McArthur seems to be. She's a milliner" Sara had continued, directing this comment to the children, "that means she makes and sells hats. When you have a chance, walk past her house and look for her sign in the picture window." The children had nodded their intent to follow Sara's suggestion.

Sara added, "When I was heading back, families were leaving the neighborhood on their way to church. As car after car passed it was clear there is indeed a benefit to having a talented milliner living in the neighborhood. I got a fashion show of men and women wearing beautiful hats I assume were created by Mrs. McArthur. As they passed, I guessed the destination of each family based upon the hat worn by the woman in the car. I predicted the women wearing the fanciest hats were headed to Baptist church services, the women wearing ornate veils were off to a Catholic church and the women wearing the least embellished hats were headed to non denominational services." Pausing, she concluded "When we're settled, I plan to ask Mrs. McArthur to make a special hat for me to wear to church."

Sara had thought about the ongoing debate she and Ben had about religion. She had been raised Lutheran and Ben had been raised Baptist. Sara had wanted to find a nice Lutheran church in the area and Ben was lukewarm on going to church at all. This was a topic added to the growing list on which Ben and Sara had failed to see eye to eye.

The remainder of their first Sunday in their new home on Julia Street was spent puttering, listening to Duke

Ellington and other favorites of Sara's while making the rooms tidy. Sara and Ben had discussed the additions they planned to make to their new home. With space already at a premium, Ben had shared with the family, "My immediate plan for the house is to add a second story with two additional bedrooms. I am also going to relocate the master bedroom to the upper level adding a picture window spanning the width of the house and featuring a small balcony. Future plans include adding a bathroom on the second floor and apartments in the rear."

Following Ben's lead, Sara had agreed with the plans for the house, the apartments in back and the timeline for completing the work. The only question was how they were going to pay for the supplies needed to make the improvements. Ben had already visited several banks requesting a loan, but none had been willing to take a chance on lending them the money. Ben decided at that point he would, "Build it if I have to pay for it one nail at a time." About that, Sara had no doubt.

Refrain:

"I Was Telling Her About You"

All neighborhoods have a rhythm and within a short time the Jamesons had settled into the groove of their new surroundings. Rather quickly Sara and Ben had gotten to know the adults on Julia Street in the way adults always have, by talking to one another. Just as Ben had imagined, Sara was in her element making new friends; asking just enough questions to show her interest and sharing just enough information to plant the seeds of intimacy.

Visits to each others' homes, chatting, playing cards and listening to music were common. Music was central to any neighborhood gathering and was the star of the show at the Jameson's home with Sara making the selections. Sara's choices were almost always Jazz featuring her favorites Duke Ellington, Ben Webster, Billie Holiday and Dizzy Gillespie. She was only too happy to provide commentary and anecdotes along with the music, which everyone had seemed to enjoy. "I'm sure I've mentioned that I went to school on the south side of Chicago at DuSable High, known primarily for its music program specializing in jazz. I was lucky enough to go to school for all four years with Nat King Cole. In my senior year Johnny Hartman showed up and we heard that Gene Ammons came in the following year as a freshman. All that talent was right there for us to enjoy during an assembly or just stopping by the music room." During these visits, Mary and Sara were building a friendship, creating a routine, carving out time to get to know each other, usually while walking through the nearby neighborhoods. Mary enjoyed Sara's anecdotes about music and Sara enjoyed Mary's stories about her family. Ben, and Mary's husband, Otis had a built in relationship based upon their shared profession, carpentry.

Making their transition to the neighborhood complete, Sara was pleased that in no time Tessa and Ronald settled in. They had gotten to know the neighborhood children in the way children always have, by playing together. Bright and early every day Ronald and Tessa joined the other young children on the block for a full day of hide and seek, jacks, jump rope, hop scotch and kick ball.

Most of the adults on Julia Street embraced the practice of taking responsibility for all of the children on the block. The children were taught to feel confident in their place in the neighborhood and in the world. Almost any adult could be counted on to come to a child's aid or mete out punishment when needed. Adults shared information freely, whether a child did well or behaved badly their parents were told right away. The children learned very early in life that everything they did mattered to someone and they were a reflection of their parents and their upbringing.

###

Just as expected, on October 12, 1943 Mary, Sara's first friend on Julia Street, welcomed her new daughter Nora into the family and the neighborhood was overflowing with well wishes and excitement. Sara and her infant son Gregory were frequent visitors at the Grabel home and it was during one of their visits when Mary had shared, "Moving to Berkeley has been bittersweet especially when I consider all the family we left; we don't have the same support here."

Sara knew exactly what Mary meant and had replied, "My family was so helpful in raising the children, I miss them so much, especially my mother. My parents are divorced and my mother is deciding what's next in her life, where she'll live and how she'll earn her living. She's looking for a fresh start."

Mary had exclaimed, "Wouldn't it be great if she moved closer, maybe even to Berkeley?"

Sara had replied without hesitation, "That would be perfect for our family, all of us."

Mary had suggested, "Maybe she can come out for a nice long visit and you can convince her to stay."

###

Momentarily shaking off the past, Sara glanced at the starburst shaped clock hanging with pride of place on the wall opposite her front door; its hands confirmed that it had been only minutes since the mailman delivered the news. Without thinking Sara touched the big white envelope as if making sure she hadn't imaged its existence. Not ready to fully acknowledge the changes that could be, she continued to look back. With no set plans for the day she allowed her memories to play on; taking her back again to 1943, fall.

Time on Julia Street had moved along mostly unnoticed. The temperature had dropped but not nearly to the degree Sara was accustomed to having lived in Chicago, and for that she had been grateful. Her new neighbors and the neighborhood became more familiar and more beautiful with each new day.

She recalled the temperature had continued dropping and the women responded by becoming more chic, their clothing and their accessories more beautiful and ornate. Perfectly tailored suits, dresses and winter coats were made from fine fabrics adorned with buttons rivaling multifaceted jewels as they reflected the light. Added to their lovely ensembles, there was an elegance to the women that was largely due to their demeanor; with the new season they stood a little taller, walked a little slower and smiled with the promise of secrets yet to unfold. Not to be outdone, the men moved through the neighborhood with long, languid almost liquid strides showcasing their beautifully fitted suits, crisp white shirts, high luster cuff links and tie clips, topped by a coordinating chapeau purchased from their neighbor the milliner, Mrs. McArthur. Appearances and fashion were very important in the Colored community and the Julia Street residents were very much in step with the times.

Eager to make new friends, Sara and Ben joined a social club which was made up of couples from around the Bay Area. Their group included fifteen couples, most lived in the Oakland Hills. Similar social groups had sprung up across the country as a means for Colored people to socialize at venues where they were welcomed and accepted. Ben and Sara's group held monthly meetings in the members' homes. At that time the highlight of the club calendar was the semi-formal and formal dances held twice a year, once in the spring and the other during the holidays. Preparing for the events had been a pleasure for Sara as she always knew what looked good on her and what she liked. Sara selected her dresses from a familiar palette, she favored cocktail and formal dresses made of luxurious fabrics in shades of green which draped easily over her 5'9" frame. Sara tended to choose silk or crepe as they slid on silently where taffeta had a voice of its own.

During those years there had been a strict protocol for dressing appropriately for every occasion, with formal events being most well defined. Ben in his tux and Sara in her cocktail dress or floor length gown, the Jamesons embraced the protocol and made a pretty picture.

Folding her feet underneath her as she lounged on the sofa, Sara smiled as she recalled her preparations for their first holiday season on Julia Street. Fall had waited silently for winter as the landscape changed from lush, full and colorful, to spare, stark and subdued, allowing the holidays to take center stage.

Like most households, Thanksgiving had always been a treasured day in the Jameson household. Of course, they all loved the fellowship with family and other invited guests, but the star of the day was the food. The family had particularly looked forward to Sara's sweet potato pie, enjoyed in most Colored homes in place of the standard pumpkin pie. Sara remembered she had stood in the kitchen listening to Ella Fitzgerald while preparing her pies as Ronald, at her side, questioned her about the ingredients. As if it were today Sara heard Ronald inquire, "What's in the sweet potato pies?"

Sara had replied, "You need sweet potatoes, butter, sugar, brown sugar, nutmeg, cinnamon, milk, eggs and vanilla."

Ronald asked for more detail, "How much of each thing do you need?"

"To taste," she had replied.

"How do you know how much?" Ronald persisted.

Sara replied, "You just know."

"I don't know!" said Ronald somewhat perturbed.

And so it went until Ronald left or was playfully asked to leave the kitchen.

At that point, the Jamesons had no financial wealth or pricey material things to pass on to their children but they had rich traditions in the form of favorite foods, abundant memories, and strong core values. They took themselves, their beliefs, and their place in the world very seriously. They, like others in the neighborhood, had always maximized whatever they had; they dressed to look

36

their best, their homes, no matter how modest, were well-kept, and the children were viewed a as an extension of themselves.

The Jameson's small dining room which adjoined the living room at that time, housed a small table set with a small bouquet of flowers as a nod to the occasion. The serving pieces and glassware purchased since their move to Berkeley sat comfortably on Sara's table. The place of honor in the middle of the table had remained empty until filled by Sara's turkey with all the trimmings. All was well when the meal had been served, blessings were said, and everyone had enjoyed the day in the new neighborhood, again reinforcing their decision to move to Berkeley.

Delighted to be a part of the holiday celebrations on Julia Street, Sara joined the neighborhood tradition of decorating their homes for the season on the day after Thanksgiving. At the same time, she started a few traditions of her own. She got up while it was still dark, left the house as soon as the street car had begun running to go down to a tree lot near Gilman Street to select the family Christmas tree. She would have the owner of the lot deliver the tree as their first delivery of the day.

On her way home from the tree lot Sara would stop in downtown Berkeley and slowly take in the scenery of the season. She enjoyed the feel of the cool crisp air and the quiet before the city was fully engaged. The moments she spent alone were among her most treasured times. Of course, she loved her family and the sounds of a family, but a few minutes alone were all Sara needed to recharge and be ready to face the day.

Buttoning her coat and tightening her favorite red knit scarf (which her mother had made) against the chill, Sara went from store front to store front, allowing herself to be fully drawn into the fantasies that were created: winter wonderland, Santa in his workshop surrounded by his elves, Mrs. Claus reading the naughty and nice list, Frosty straightening his hat. Sara had been taken by the detail; the scenes took her breath away, much like she felt whenever she heard a beautiful piece of music. After appreciating the moment, Sara was ready to start back home.

Sara loved to walk, either alone or with the children. Whenever time and distance were not an issue, walking was her preferred mode of transportation. She also enjoyed riding the trolley. Ben did not share Sara's love of walking; he preferred to drive a car, saying that he had gotten his fill of walking and riding public transportation in his younger years.

As expected, the Christmas holidays had sparkled on Julia Street. Every home boasted an evergreen tree trimmed with colorful glass ornaments, silver tinsel and red and green lights. At each home the living room drapes remained open and the freshly washed windows were brightly lit to allow the holiday cheer to be visible from the street. There was a festive uniformity from one home to the next, a "sameness" that was perfect for the neighborhood.

The exceptions were the Simpson and McArthur homes. These homeowners took holiday décor to a different level. Mrs. Simpson had appeared to struggle with being ostentatious and tasteful at the same time, seeming to walk the thin line between being showy and being a showoff. Starting with the wreath on her front door, Mrs. Simpson used white, gold and silver glass balls, garlands and ribbon to enhance all of her decorations. Everything as far as the eye could see was liberally sprinkled with crystals for good measure. All was high quality and high impact.

Right next door Mrs. McArthur had called on her considerable talent rather than just her checkbook to create an Alice in Wonderland Christmas, successfully incorporating her gorgeous hats into her holiday theme. Each of the more recognizable fairytale characters, Alice, The Mad Hatter, The White Rabbit, The Cheshire Cat and The Queen of Hearts, wore a wonderful hat created by Mrs. McArthur just for the holidays. The display was simply beautiful and so fitting for the holidays and for the woman of the house. Mrs. McArthur was tall and elegant; she wore her hats well and she was an excellent advertisement for her creations. This had been her season to shine, her talents very much on display.

The Christmas season was punctuated by neighborhood gatherings, the celebration moved from one home to another. The parties were fun for the entire family; beautiful decorations with the Christmas tree as the focal point, cocktails and hors d'oeuvres for the adults, punch and finger foods for the children and if they were really lucky, a visit from the man of the hour, Santa. With the possibility of Santa attending, the children were on their best behavior, at least for the duration of the party.

While it was clear the hosts had put considerable time and resources into the ambiance, food, and drink, the highlight of each gathering was the company. The people on Julia Street had enjoyed getting dressed up, they had enjoyed each other and the time they spent together. As the festive evenings had worn on, the children, worn out, were sent home with an overnight sitter as the adults lingered. The night time was for the adults, food and drinks were replenished as animated conversations between groups of women and groups of men gave way to music and dancing until the early morning light.

Wondering about their absence, during one of the parties Sara had observed to no one in particular, "Mr. and Mrs. Simpson have not attended or hosted any of our neighborhood parties, but I have noticed some rather elaborate affairs at their home in the last couple of weeks." Eva had replied with her customary wink, "Oh well, I guess we're just not their kind."

The parties and the holidays had ended joyfully it seemed, for everyone except Sara. For the most part Millicent had been of no consequence to Sara, she had scarcely noticed her in the neighborhood or at neighborhood gatherings. Millicent rarely mingled with other women; at parties she had a habit of standing in a remote corner surrounded by a group of male admirers. Millicent and her habits were of no consequence to Sara until the last party of the season where Millicent's group of admirers had dwindled to one, Ben.

"I Could Have Told You"

Neighborhood gossip hung in the air like a fine mist. Millicent, who had never been a favorite in the eyes of the Julia Street women, was the main topic; she had ended her on-again, off-again marriage. Before the night of the holiday party, whenever Sara had thought of Millicent (which was rare) she recalled move-in day when Millicent had joined the group of women assembled to welcome the Jamesons and Grabels to the neighborhood. Although Millicent was less than friendly, Sara had been unfazed, thinking instead of a phrase her father used often, "one monkey don't stop no show." Sara had chosen to focus on the warm welcome she and Mary received from the other women in the neighborhood, rendering Millicent harmless. Since the party, Sara didn't know what to think of Millicent, but she thought of her often. In the short time Sara had known Millicent, Sara had heard her say to anyone who would listen, "I think it's best to collect vices one at a time." It was evident she had already mastered drinking and smoking and had moved on to collecting men. According to Millicent's rules, since her divorce *all* the Julia Street men were possible contestants for her new dating game. She had chosen the neighborhood holiday parties to debut "New year, new men," which seemed to be her post divorce motto. In Sara's view Millicent's new motto hadn't been very different than her pre-divorce behavior.

One afternoon shortly after the holidays, gathered at Eva's home, some of the women from the neighborhood had spent several hours trying to figure out, among other things, exactly what men saw in Millicent. They sat comfortably in Eva's living room, a showcase for objects that anyone with children would never dream of owning. Eva's home was tasteful, extravagant and just a little decadent, very much an extension of the woman who lived there.

Much to the delight of her guests, Eva was a gracious hostess who excelled at making everyone feel special and right at home. "Okay ladies," Eva had announced affably, "It's your choice; I will serve you if that makes you happy or you may serve yourself if that is your preference." Given free rein to enjoy themselves, they took pleasure in their surroundings; the chance to chat and listen to good music, including selections by Billie Holiday, Arthur Prysock and Dinah Washington.

Each woman had felt free to express an opinion about anything, but most of the conversation was focused on Millicent. After a lively debate, they agreed she must have been attractive in a way that was not visible to the naked eye and also surmised that she had a way about her that was not understandable to other women.

After compiling a rather lengthy list of Millicent's

faults, it was unanimous that her most irritating habit was her behavior at neighborhood gatherings. She invariably came in late wearing one of her completely inappropriate outfits, then picking a remote corner of the room separating herself from the other women so that she could be surrounded by a group of men. There were always men who were willing to oblige.

The women had expanded on some of Millicent's other faults aloud.

"She talks about her endless beauty treatments which, by the way, don't seem to be working that well. Seems like she spends a lot of time and money for not a lot of results, she never changes. Perhaps someone, maybe you Eva, should tell her that if she is going to try to be so hoity toity she needs to stop sounding like she's just off the farm. Please inform her that Easter eggs are dyed, hair is colored. Chickens are plucked and eyebrows are shaped. Easy mistakes but she's just tacky and irritating."

"She doesn't walk, she traipses. She traipses through the neighborhood in a questionable outfit with her ever present cocktail in hand, descending upon her neighbor's homes without warning or invitation. She never stays very long, especially if the man of the house isn't there."

Not really participating but taking it all in, Sara had silently admitted that on balance, Millicent and her many flaws had been only of mild concern to her, but that all changed at the last party of the holiday season.

One more thing that had been filed away for later.

###

A light knock on the front door brought Sara back to the here and now. Not bothering to ask "who's there," she opened the door to find Leona who had been her friend since the day Sara arrived at the South Berkeley boarding house all those years ago. Leona never changed; her smile was still bright and beautiful, she still knew everything and everybody and was all too eager to dish with Sara. Surprisingly-given how much Leona loved to talk, she never gossiped; she talked about events and ideas or people that she cared about.

Certain there was no particular reason for the visit Sara opened the door wide, greeting her friend with a smile. Leona was pretty with a dark brown complexion, big beautiful brown eyes and sable hair, a compact figure and a smile so warm it was almost startling.

"Leona, come on in. I'm not doing much of anything, just sitting here with my thoughts."

"Girl, I guess I came just in time. You know how dangerous thinking can be," replied Leona, both of them laughing.

"Sit down while I get us a fresh cup of coffee," said Sara as she made her way into the kitchen. Leona made herself at home and in no time Sara was back with two mugs of black coffee.

No matter how hard she tried to forget, whenever they got together Sara recalled "that visit" from Leona shortly after Sara's family moved to Julia Street. If history is a reliable witness, it is a visit Sara's not likely to forget. That day it seemed as if Leona had feared she was the bearer of bad news; right away Sara had known something was wrong. Leona's body language and lack of eye contact said that she would have preferred to be anywhere other than Sara's living room. Quickly Sara had reasoned why Leona was there. Sparing her the discomfort of having to share too many details, Sara recalled trying to seem unfazed by saying, "Thank you for your concern Leona but that issue has been resolved." Leona had been visibly relieved and had attempted to shift all of the "blame" onto Millicent, "the perpetual other woman". Sara had appreciated Leona's efforts to render Ben blameless but Sara had closed down that line of conversation as well. Time revealed that Millicent hadn't been the problem after all.

"What's new?" asked Leona, accepting her coffee cup as Sara joined her on the sofa. Knowing her so well, Sara could tell by Leona's cheerful manner the visit was just to pass the time.

Ready to chat but not ready to share the contents of the envelope she'd received earlier in the mail, Sara replied "Not too much new happening here. What about with you?"

Even when Leona's answer was "nothing," she had a way of making old news seem new again. She also had a way of telling the same story but with a slightly different flavor each time. She was always happy to talk about her two grown children (both daughters) and without fail she lit up when she shared the small details of her grandchildren's lives.

Leona rarely talked about herself but in conversations years ago she had dispelled the boarding house rumor that her husband had been killed in the war, sharing with Sara that she had never been married. Leona had continued to work at the Richmond Shipyards and live in Mrs. Knight's boarding house until the war ended in 1945. She then accepted a job at the Richmond Post Office and moved into the housing left vacant after the Shipyard management had been given just three days to vacate the premises when the end of the war was announced. After the White folks moved out of the units which had been called "the projects", the name stuck. For the last ten years Leona has lived in a small duplex on King and Ashby Streets, just three blocks away from Sara. Leona successfully raised her two children and is an active, involved grandmother.

Responding to Sara's greeting Leona smiled broadly, "I'm waiting for my new grandbaby to come so I decided to get some air rather than sit by the phone. Next thing I knew I was at your door."

"I'm glad." Already knowing the answer Sara asked, "With the new baby, what's your total?"

Leona's features softened as she thought of her grandchildren, "Four-- three boys-- we're all hoping this one will be a girl." All of them were as cute as they could be evidenced by the snapshots Leona eagerly shared. Pulling out the latest photos, Leona was off and running. She shared pictures and information freely, some more than once but that never bothered Sara; she enjoyed Leona's stories and her company. The two friends talked about their children, grandchildren, their jobs and life in general.

The visit ended as abruptly as it began with Leona

taking her mug into the kitchen, talking as she walked. "I better get back home I don't want to miss the call. I'll keep you posted."

Before Sara could say much more than "Good luck with the baby," Leona was out the door and down the front steps-- leaving Sara to think of her own grandchildren and how delighted she had been with the arrival of each one.

Over twenty years ago when Sara had moved out of Mrs. Knight's boarding house, she had been almost certain she and Leona would never see each other again, each with good intentions but sure life would take them in different directions. Sara never imagined how important Leona would become to her. She felt indebted to Leona for taking such an interest in Sara's family-- their happiness and well being when they first moved to Berkeley. She had also been charmed by Leona's efforts to help her save face all those years ago. Ever since, there has been a mutual effort to grow the relationship into a full-blown friendship spanning many years.

Leona's visits never failed to remind Sara of the early days in Berkeley. Leona had been her first friend in a new town; making the transition so much easier for Sara and her family. Talk of the new baby reminded Sara of her first year on Julia Street with an infant of her own.

She had been planning to go back to work but she didn't know anyone in the neighborhood well enough to allow them to care for Gregory, who at that time was less than a year old. The two of them had been visiting in Mary's living room just weeks after Mary delivered her daughter Nora when Mary told Sara, "My maternity leave is ending and I'm expected back at work by the middle of

January." In response, Sara shared her plans to return to work as well. They discussed their need for daycare and the fact that each of them had decided to turn to their mothers for help.

Mary had shared excitedly, "My mother will stay with us during the week, she will come on Sunday evening and go back home for the weekends."

Sara smiled, "That's wonderful. My story isn't all happy; our opportunity is born out of my parents' sadness, they have divorced and my mother wants a new start. We were delighted to offer her a place in our home for as long as she wants to stay and she has accepted. She is coming from Chicago by train and will be here at the end of this week."

Sara recalled that at that point she and Mary were preparing for their return to work in little more than a week, Mary taking her position at the Veterans Administration in Oakland and Sara starting as a Postal Clerk at the main Post Office in downtown Berkeley. To be ready for their new jobs they had planned a long overdue shopping trip to add a few pieces of post-baby clothing and accessories to their wardrobes. On the morning of the planned outing Sara had awakened early and realized how excited she was to have a girl's day with Mary. She had hurriedly made all of the preparations necessary to be away from home for most of the day including provisions for Gregory and the older children. Sara had gotten dressed quickly and then made her way down the block to Mary's home. Sara found Mary waiting restlessly on the front porch, when she saw Sara she skipped down the stairs to meet her as they chuckled at their own excitement.

They had dressed carefully in day dresses, walking heels, nylons and appropriate accessories. They knew how important it was to present the right image, particularly as Colored women shopping in the better stores. They had chatted a little bit about the difficulty of being away from home for an entire day and how much preparation it had taken to make it happen.

Sara had remarked, "I'm so grateful my mother arrived in time. Imagine how hard it would be if our mothers were not here."

Mary replied, "I'm pretty sure it would be impossible, just think of our husbands taking care of the children and the house for a full day." That thought had brought a laugh and a tiny shudder.

Mary and Sara had always looked forward to a walk through Berkeley; they felt comfortable walking almost anywhere in the city. Every neighborhood had its own distinct personality made apparent by the landscaping, the styles and colors of the homes and the cars the residents drove. It was fun for Mary and Sara to imagine what kind of people lived in the homes as they passed.

On many of their walks Sara and Mary talked about the city, the attitudes of the people and how for the most part, as Colored women they felt accepted by White people. It had not escaped their notice that they lived almost entirely separate lives from the White population in town. The South Berkeley neighborhood Mary and Sara lived in was almost entirely Colored and they rarely, if ever, went into areas where White people lived. In most cases the only interaction they had with White people was at their jobs and when they ran errands outside of their own neighborhood.

Most times, when shopping, they were welcomed by White sales people, but it was common for a store clerk to call out, "Who's next?" or to wait on the White customer when they knew full well Mary or Sara was next in line. That's just the way it was, racism had been woven into the fabric of their daily lives. But if the service was not to their liking, they had simply shopped elsewhere.

On this occasion their conversation had been totally upbeat. Walking down California Street Sara had suggested, as they were turning right onto Russell, "Let's walk down to Grove Street so that we can walk past Berkeley High School." Mary had eagerly agreed. Berkeley High was the only public high school in town; it had been well respected and known as the place the University of California professors sent their children to school. What Mary didn't know was that Sara had a closely held hope that one day she would attend U. C. Berkeley fulfilling her goal of becoming a college graduate.

While passing the impressive high school Mary had declared aloud, "Just think, our children will be Berkeley High graduates."

Sara enthusiastically replied, "Absolutely, especially since it is the only game in town and as neither of us plan to move away, I guarantee they will all be Berkeley High grads and then off to U.C. Berkeley they'll go."

That settled, before they knew it they had

walked and chatted their way to Hink's in downtown Berkeley.

Hink's was a utilitarian department store, not overly fancy, which catered to middle-aged, middle-classed White women, but when shopping for work appropriate clothing it was a good bet they would find what was needed. Mary and Sara enjoyed trying on outfits and window shopping together. There was never any competition selecting clothing as they had two distinct body types; Mary at five foot three was very petite and Sara at five foot nine was not. They had developed a short hand in order to save time; a quick shake of the head meant *don't even bother trying it on*, where an enthusiastic nod meant *add it to the try on pile*. When each of them had accumulated the total number of items allowed in the dressing room, they went in and only came out when an outfit was a definite maybe. After a quick review of their options and finding nothing that truly fit the bill, Sara suggested they take the street car into downtown Oakland where the shopping options were vast and varied.

Riding the streetcar had allowed them the opportunity to visit with each other, finalize their shopping lists and see the sights while someone else did the driving. The women had regularly relied on the Key System for transportation in town and when going to Oakland. Whenever they went to San Francisco from Berkeley or Oakland they had taken the ferry or more infrequently one of them drove.

Sara said to Mary, "I am planning to buy a brown wool pleated skirt to wear with my brown and tan wool jacket. You know the one, with the padded shoulders and the gorgeous jeweled button at the waist. Also, I will look for the perfect shade of red lipstick, the accessory I can always afford."

Mary shared, "I've already had a few of my skirts shortened to the knee, the new style we talked about, but I need a few pair of nylons."

"Oh Mary, I almost forgot, my one vice - perfume. I will definitely get a small bottle of My Sin or Evening in Paris. I never leave the house without a dab of one or the other."

Arriving at the center of the shopping district in Oakland, Mary had proposed as she glanced up and down Broadway, "Let's take a quick turn through Capwell's and Goldman's, and end our day over at I Magnin."

Sara had quickly agreed saying, "It's not as glamorous as downtown San Francisco but the better stores are lush and luxurious. Just being inside each store is a treat." Not entirely a treat if you happened to be Negro. Sara was reminded of the day she and Tessa had gone shopping in downtown San Francisco. They had been looking for a few things but at the fancier stores they were window shopping. They had walked into City of Paris where they stood just taking in the beauty of the store. As they made their way down the perfume aisle **all** of the sales ladies had stopped what they were doing and stared at Sara and Tessa. Sara was accustomed to this reaction but it was new to Tessa who was not a seasoned shopper. Alarmed, Tessa grabbed Sara's hand and whispered "why are they staring at us?" Sara had replied in her normal tone of voice "They are staring at us because we're gorgeous." Sara had then swept over to the counter where her favorite fragrance was displayed, took the tester, spritzed herself and Tessa and then left the store. Every time Sara thought of that afternoon she was hopeful that Tessa had believed her explanation.

Mary and Sara were prudent shoppers who knew which styles were most flattering and appropriate for the workplace. Throughout their girls day the women had fondled fabric to determine comfort and durability, checked tags for sizes and prices and eventually tried on items that made the cut. Ultimately, each of them had bought a few things to enhance their work wardrobes, including complimentary accessories and cosmetics.

Nudging Sara, Mary reminded her that a day of shopping in downtown Oakland would not be complete without a stop at Kress' candy counter, known for its assortment of warm nuts and creamy chocolates. "Kress would be a perfect stop at the end of the day." agreed Sara.

Feeling a little tired but victorious by day's end, with packages in hand, they had arrived back in the neighborhood just in time for their hair appointments in Sara's next door neighbor, Eva's, kitchen. Sara was very fond of Eva. She had demonstrated through her many kindnesses how much she enjoyed living next door to Sara and her family.

Sara found herself smiling as she remembered the morning she had stood at her front door with it slightly ajar so that she could see and hear her children while they played outside. She recalled hearing Eva say to Tessa and Ronald, "What is your favorite color? I 'm adding a few flowers to my garden and I want to make sure you like them." This had not been an isolated incident nor was it for Sara's benefit. Eva was warm and welcoming to the entire Jameson family, especially to Sara's children which was a key to Sara's heart.

As a proven expert Eva had been entrusted with almost every woman's hair in the neighborhood with Sara and Mary only too happy to join the group. Prior to arriving on Eva's doorstep they had discussed their desired treatments and preferred hairstyles. Eva didn't require much direction as she completely understood style and fashion and always looked fabulous. She changed her hairstyle and makeup at the drop of a hat and encouraged others to keep their look current but be true to who they were at their core. Her favorite saying was, "Styles change. Style doesn't."

When asked, Mary had explained to Eva, "We want a hairstyle that looks great with minimal fuss. Remember we have brand new babies, older children, a husband, a house, and a job. Need I say more?"

Eva had replied with a smile, "Just like every woman who sits in my chair."

Before either of them had a chance to sit down, Eva had insisted Mary and Sara model at least one of their new outfits, she said, "To get more of a sense of the look each wanted to achieve." The women happily agreed.

Mary, in a new midnight blue suit with gorgeous silver and lapis buttons and Sara, in a lovely ecru silk blouse with an elongated bow at the v-necked collar paired with her new jacket, each had looked as if she were ready to take on their new challenges. Eva remarked how stylish they looked and raved about the cut and color of their outfits, assuring them their new hairdos would be their crowning glory.

Two hours later they were pleased with their new looks and were very complimentary of Eva and her skills as a beautician and magician. While still admiring each other's new hairstyles and expressing how happy they were with the day, they had encountered Mrs. Simpson as they were leaving Eva's home. Of course, Mrs. Simpson was inquisitive about their day and the contents of their shopping bags. Sara and Mary were secretly pleased their purchases were from the more prestigious downtown Oakland stores of I Magnin and Goldman's.

As they were passing, Mrs. Simpson said, "I hear you are both returning to work." Turning to Sara she asked "I'm curious, what exactly does one wear while performing the duties of a U.S. postal clerk?"

Sara, recognizing Mrs. Simpson's rude intent, replied with a question of her own, "Do you mean in addition to the flag?"

That evening Sara had a full night of work ahead of her. After accepting the new job at the Post Office Sara had spent her free time *pitching her scheme*; practicing tossing mail by address and zones into a cardboard mockup of her work area. Postal zones, usually one or two digits at the time and included as part of the address, had been created after the start of the World War II. With so many of the regular mail clerks serving their country at the time, their replacements had trouble sorting the mail without additional information.

Sara had set up her practice area in the living room and the children had been happy to assist her in any way that they could, usually by creating stacks of "mail" (pieces of papers with made up names and addresses) before she pitched them into the correct slots. Sara had easily met both the accuracy and time requirements when she was tested before being offered the job, but she wanted to make sure she was well practiced on her first day of work.

The days passed quickly and too soon Sara started her new job at the Downtown Berkeley Post Office. After a short while Sara and the family had fallen into a routine and soon it was as if Sara had never left the workforce at all. Fortunately, Sara's mother had assumed her role as care giver, supplier of good meals and valued member of the Jameson household. Mrs. Crawford also adapted to the routine nicely, creating a sense of calm and order simply with her presence.

With Sara working at the Post Office and Ben a skilled carpenter in a growing city with lots of building projects, employment should not have been an issue. On a daily basis Ben used the Carpenter's Local Union Hall located on University Avenue in downtown Berkeley as his primary resource for finding new jobs. The Union Hall was where the match was made between employers and potential employees using a pre-qualified list of candidates. There were specific requirements for remaining a member of the union in good standing and Ben had met them. The written rule was that all assignments were made by seniority. The *reality* was that all assignments were made by seniority and race. White males, regardless of seniority, had been placed at the top of the list sometimes displacing those who should have been hired. That's just the way it was. Whenever Ben did not have a paying job he made additions and improvements to his own property. He added a second story; he said to house his children, and three rental apartments in back. He was happy to be able to do it.

The additional space to the Jameson's home had filled up fast. A room was used for Sara's mother, Mrs. Crawford, and another for the new baby that was expected in January 1945 which at that point was just a few months away.

"Good Morning Heartache"

Still sitting in the same spot on the sofa Sara told herself her extended stay in the past had lasted long enough; she needed to make a decision about the contents of the large white envelope. As she usually did when faced with a quandary Sara went over to the console, made her selections, stacked her choices on the spindle, turned on the record player and settled in. Reaching for the envelope, taking out a single sheet of paper re-reading the first lines, Sara thought of the last time she had been made a similar offer. All those years ago when she was a senior in high school, in spite of being offered a full scholarship to her first choice University, there had not been enough money available even for the train fare. It was different this time; she was an almost fifty year old woman with money of her own, who lived so close to the University of California at Berkeley she could walk to class.

The letter read "We are delighted to offer you provisional* admission for the 1967 Summer Session." The asterisk seemed to suggest there was a problem; perhaps the time that had elapsed between her stellar high school performance and graduation in 1937, and her anticipated start at UC Berkeley some thirty years later, might be problematic. It further suggested that perhaps there was a chance she might not be successful but Sara had no doubt that she would do well. Sara signed the letter accepting their acceptance and placed it in her mailbox to be picked up the next day. She even added a stamp and a return address to the envelope something she rarely did when mailing bill payments. Sara let them pick up the fee on the other end.

With that done Sara again settled comfortably into her seat on the sofa, reading and re-reading all of the contents of the envelope and beginning to visualize herself on campus. In her excitement Sara noted key dates to the calendar that she kept on the small table next to the sofa. Sara began mentally preparing for "opening day."

Except for the music, Sara's constant companion, the house was quiet, unlike all the years when the house had been filled to the rafters. The Jameson household had always been lively, particularly when the children's or Sara's friends visited, which had been often. Added to that was Sara's music and most times it had been downright loud. Those had been good times for everyone it seemed, except Ben.

Early on Sara had been surprised that Ben was so sensitive to noise. She thought coming from a family of seven children he would be quite used to it. He had not enjoyed the neighborhood children's frequent visits, a fact he hadn't hid. As a result they had timed most of their visits to when Ben was not home. If he returned during their visit, whenever they heard his footsteps on the porch the atmosphere in the living room would change. No one could predict what kind of mood he would be in except that it would likely not be good.

When he would turn the doorknob and cross the threshold the visitors said their goodbyes. As they had made their way to the door they said, "Hi Mr. Jameson nice to see you. Sorry, but we were just leaving." Ben would walk through the living room where everyone was gathered and up the stairs to the bedroom he had built for himself and Sara.

Because Ben Jameson was hard to know, few people were aware of how smart he was, particularly in math and science; how creative, intuitive and sensitive he was. Few ever saw him lovingly stroke Tessa's hair as she sat at his feet while he read the newspaper and she read a book, or the quiet times he shared with Sara in companionable conversation about nothing in particular. He had kept most of his thoughts and words to himself, except the angry ones.

Ben had a quick temper, no one ever knew what might set him off; he was like a string stretched too taut. There was a randomness about him. He would show up at varying times without warning as if trying to catch everyone off guard and perhaps trick them into interacting with him in a different more positive way.

Sara was surprised by just how much Ben didn't like music. In front of everyone he often made his feelings known, stating "I don't care if any of them ever play another note," to someone else it could have seemed small but it was huge. This cruel revelation had broken Sara's heart every time.

Ben was prickly, unpredictable, secretive, and absent.

Sara was solitary, cutting, unforgiving, remote and unresponsive.

At that point in the marriage Ben and Sara were developing patterns that could become so deeply ingrained that they would be hard to dismantle, if they ever wanted to.

Of course their relationship impacted the children. The girls had managed to stay out of the fray but Ben had been particularly tough on his sons, Ronald and Gregory, perhaps because he felt they were nothing like him. Gregory was an artist at heart, and in fact, he would take a piece of paper, a length of string or a lump of clay and turn them into treasures. He worked in graphite, colored pencil, charcoal and oils on paper and canvas creating brilliant pieces, some as large as three- feet by nine-feet, mostly abstracts. His best friend also named Gregory was not a big fan of the abstracts and had often jokingly suggested he "just paint a big horse." Ronald was a thinker, very measured in word and deed. He excelled in math and science, was excellent with people and fiercely loyal to those he cared about. No doubt Ben thought his job was to toughen up Ronald and Gregory before they went out into the world but if he had looked a little closer he would have seen the qualities the three of them had in common and seen that his sons were plenty tough already.

From the start Sara had been aware of the dynamics between her husband and her sons and would attempt to balance the scales by being extra kind to the boys and even icier with Ben. Sara had been determined that her sons would be valued in her home and heart, if nowhere else. This "favoritism" was not lost on Ben and had most likely fueled his displeasure. It was a sad and angry dance. Ben began to spend more time alone upstairs in the master bedroom or away from home, presumably at the pool hall or the tiny night club on Sacramento Street. More and more while shopping in the neighborhood Sara took notice of the pool hall and night club and the small group of men who stood in front. With growing unease she had often found Ben among them.

There had been a trigger, not catastrophic unless you call two people who had broken each others' hearts over and over catastrophic. Sara loved music, Ben didn't. Sara enjoyed company, Ben didn't. Ben enjoyed quiet, Sara didn't. Sara coddled her sons, Ben didn't. Sara was a homebody, Ben wasn't. Added to all that, Sacramento Street and the women; there was the trigger. For some time Sara felt as if she were becoming someone she didn't recognize or respect which was watchful, distrustful, unkind and unsteady. Not a woman she would want her daughters to become or her sons to marry.

The last straw had been a phone call. It was either late night or early morning. Sara had been sitting in her spot on the sofa singing along with Billie Holiday as she often did when the house was still.

Without even looking at the clock, somehow Sara knew it was a call after last-call. Sara had imagined that all of the drinks had been served, consumed and people had begun to think about going home or to someone else's home. It's likely that's when the unpleasantness had begun.

Sara had stopped her imagining and answered the telephone. Because of the background noise she had only made out a few of the words but she had gotten the message, "Been hurt, Highland Hospital, on the way there now."

Sara's mother and children had been awakened by the ringing telephone and had insisted on knowing what was going on. Giving them the barest of details, details even more sketchy than the information she had been given, she assured them everything would be all right. She told them not to worry, to go back to bed and she would contact or see them as soon as she was able.

As always, careful of the impression she would make, Sara had taken a minute to freshen up before leaving the house. When she arrived at the hospital Sara approached the nurse's station. "I'm Sara Jameson. I'm looking for my husband, Benjamin Jameson."

The nurse had responded, "Your husband's condition is not life-threatening and he will be released within the hour. For more information you will need to talk to the doctor."

After thanking the nurse for her help Sara was then directed to the doctor who had attended her husband. When they met, it appeared to Sara that the doctor had regarded her with a casualness that did not fit the seriousness of the occasion. He had introduced himself and by way of explanation he said simply, with an expression Sara could have only characterize as a smirk,

"Well, these situations seem to escalate when there is alcohol, men and women." He had said it as if in Sara's world "these situations" were to be expected and she was expected to anticipate and accept them.

Clearly, Sara knew the doctor's attitude toward her and her husband was not the only thing wrong with the situation, but it had been the catalyst that led her to change her perspective on this and all the other situations that she had routinely accepted.

In that moment, informed by the casual ease with which the doctor had categorized so many women and Sara, she had done an accounting of herself and her marriage; she hadn't liked what she'd seen.

In that moment Sara had been reminded of all the ways she and Ben were different; big and small. She had relived the slights both real and imagined. She recalled the solitude, self imposed or due to Ben's absences and his time spent on Sacramento Street. But mostly she thought of the women. Sara had not been jealous or even angry about the women, she had mostly been sad. Not so much that there were other women, but by the circumstances surrounding them. She had been saddened that she knew of their existence; that her feelings had not mattered enough for Ben to make sure that she hadn't known about them.

In that moment Sara acknowledged that many things about her marriage were sad and topping the list was Ben's constant choosing. Sara needed the choices to be already made, things settled and decided. Ben needed things to be fluid and open ended, with options yet to consider. Once married, Sara thought the choosing had already been done; she thought she had been chosen, once and for all. But Ben had continued choosing, again and again.

Sara had been most saddened by the women Ben chose; they seemed flimsy, frivolous, directionless and buffeted. They were unattached, unencumbered, detached, fancy free. Sara was none of those things; she was sturdy, directed, tethered, affiliated, anchored, part of a packaged deal with a matched set, two girls and two boys.

Ben had a type and Sara wasn't it.

On that note, Sara had thanked the doctor for his medical attention and she had silently thanked him for the chance to be viewed through a stranger's eyes. In that moment Sara changed.

Sara was taken to her husband and was unsettled by his appearance, but at the same time grateful his injuries were not more extensive. They had sat for a short while and at the appointed time he was discharged. Sara had driven Ben home with only minimal conversation.

Out of concern and obligation, true to form, Sara had icily inquired "Are you all right? What exactly happened?" knowing her tone and manner would signal how she felt.

Ben, no stranger to conflict, had answered tersely, "I'm fine it's no big deal."

"No big deal", Sara had replied in disbelief, "To get a call in the middle of the night, alarming everyone in the household, from someone I don't know, instructing me to go to Highland Hospital NOW because my husband has been hurt, that's NO BIG DEAL? I find it an incredibly big deal."

Ben's responses were barely audible and abrupt, non-answers and brusque apologies. Sara had made no response. This was their dance. When Sara was angry, frightened or upset, she withheld her words while radiating her disapproval. Ben became more prickly and combative - his go-to response when he was not sure of a better way. Ben rarely took the time to plan his responses he simply reacted, often to his detriment; that night had been a prime example.

Ben had been truly sorry and wished he had been able to share his feelings with Sara but he was hardly able to admit them to himself. He was frightened by the damage done to their relationship, ashamed of his contribution to their pain and jealous, jealous of Sara's music. He knew it was "silly" to be jealous of a "thing" but the way the music transformed her and took her to a place that did not include him made him sad, angry and insecure. Even at that moment when he most needed to, he could not say it out loud so he sat there falling deeper into the rut that widened the expanse between them.

When they got home Sara's mother and the children were relieved and everyone went to sleep. The next few days found Ben at home, on the mend, but the pull back to the scene of the incident proved magnetic, much to everyone's dismay and Sara's disappointment. Despite the tragedy that could have been, nothing had changed, except Sara's tolerance.

Shortly after his recovery, Ben moved out of the house on Julia Street where he had built the upstairs rooms to house his children, relocated the master bedroom and where he had added the large picture window and the small balcony.

After the move he still showed up at random times and in that regard, too, he had not changed.

Second Verse:

"Fine and Mellow"

They all knew the story. Years ago Ben and Sara had forged a connection across the gulf of their life experiences, two very different people from very different backgrounds who had agreed on next to nothing. Nobody other than the two of them could say exactly how they had met or why they believed they would be a good match, but the answers to those questions had taken on far less importance since Ben had moved out of the house on Julia Street.

Since the move, Ben and Sara were free from questions that had no answers and from expectations that would never be met.

Since the move, Ben and Sara were not different people but they saw each other in a different light.

Since the move, Sara and Ben behaved with the freedom of two people who had been released from roles they had never learned and perhaps should never have been asked to play.

"Come Dance With Me"

Sara got dressed with ease and efficiency; she was accustomed to her "work uniform" having worn it for years. As she dressed for her day, she selected a slim fitted skirt that hit just below the knee with a coordinating blouse according to the fashion of the day, adding nylons and shoes with a chunky two-inch heel. Finishing her preparations she carefully added a dab of perfume, a touch of lipstick, her favorite earrings and her only wristwatch with the small diamonds and rubies, the one her father had sent for her birthday years earlier. Her wedding ring had long since been stored in a jewelry box.

Sara had taken a job at the Oakland Army Base after Patrice, her youngest was born. For years while her children were young Sara's mother had made it possible for her to work with little worry for their well being, she knew her children had been in the best possible hands. Now that they were all grown up with children of their own their day to day well being was no longer an issue but always a concern.

Even after all this time, Sara enjoys her job at the Base and the people she works with. Her role as a Freight Analyst is challenging and takes advantage of skills she doesn't even know she has. She learns new things every day and feels she is making a contribution.

Not many people know the Oakland Army Base was considered a major transportation hub where upwards of 7 million tons of cargo moved in and out during World War II and was equipped to handle at least that volume into the foreseeable future.

Sara knew she thrived on organization; for so long while living in a home with three adults, four children and one bathroom they had been called on to be unselfish and extremely organized in order to get out on time in the mornings. To this day on Monday through Friday Sara was up by 6:00 a.m., bathed, dressed and out of the door by 6:10 a.m. She met her carpool on the Northwest corner of Sacramento Street and Ashby Avenue in front of the gas station at 6:20 a.m., allowing Sara and her colleagues to be at their desks in plenty of time to start their work day at 7:00 a.m.

This would be Sara's last Friday on day shift as well as her last day riding in the car pool; school was starting on the following Monday. She had been granted a transfer to swing shift which meant in addition to her school challenges she would also be driving herself to work something she had not done before.

Sara's last shift on days was filled with goodbyes and good wishes.

"Don't be a stranger Sara. We're gonna miss your music recommendations, we'll just have to come to your house and hear them first hand."

Most everyone from the day shift she would see at least in passing when the shifts changed but the few that were her friends she would see often.

As she was riding home for the last time in the car pool Sara thought not for the first time since making the decision to go back to school, that she was a forty-seven year old woman, long-time separated from her husband, working mother of four adult children, grandmother of three and as of Monday a college student. Arriving at her stop, as she got out of the car she bid her colleagues a good weekend and thanked them for the memories. Sara took the short walk down Sacramento Street turning right onto Julia, finding her way home.

The weekend took on a cadence of its own as Sara divided her time between visits from friends and family and planning for the start of school. On Sunday Sara went to church. Years earlier she had found a Lutheran church in Oakland which her family (including Ben, sometimes) had attended for years. Sara relied on Pastor Kline for his cool, calm counsel on many issues over the years. It never failed to create a sense of calm in Sara as he prayed the benediction, "May the Lord bless you and keep you. May He turn His face toward you and give you His peace," at the end of the service each week. He would say this as he walked down the center aisle to greet each parishioner as they left the sanctuary.

After church Sara took a dry-run drive through downtown Berkeley up to the campus in search of the parking structure closest to her first class. As she got closer to Telegraph Avenue the tone and tenor of the atmosphere changed from quiet suburban neighborhoods to frenetic eclectic "meet, greet and shop" hangouts. The sidewalks were lined with people buying and vendors selling t-shirts, silver jewelry, leather goods and all manner of tie-dyed apparel. Sara found her parking destination, parked the car and walked across campus. It was a gorgeous day in mid June at mid day. The temperature was mild, the sky was clear and the 'hippies' were out in full force in all their splendor. They wore tie-dyed, head bands, blue jeans, tunic tops and sandals in all colors, and not just the females. Sara could hardly wait for the next day.

As she strolled down the footpath toward Sproul Hall Sara let her mind wander down a different path. Years ago Sara and Ben had held Tessa out of school for a year so that she and Ronald could start school together, Tessa in first grade and Ronald in kindergarten. Sara smiled as she thought of Tessa in her pretty cotton dress, pastel cardigan and saddle oxford shoes and Ronald in his crisp, creased long khaki pants and striped long-sleeved shirt. Sara and her children had joined the other Julia Street children making their way to Lincoln Elementary School. Walking at a good clip, the kids all talking at once, had shared that they looked forward to stopping on the way to school at the little grocery store. It was located right around the corner, across the street from Mrs. Crawford's good friend Bell's house, on the corners of California and Ashby. Sara had been delighted by Tessa telling her a story the older kids had shared with her; "The

Chinese people who own the store are really nice and when we walk by on the way to school and want to buy something, even if the store isn't open yet, all we have to do is knock on the door and they will come down and let us in." It had seemed that Tessa couldn't think of a nicer way to start the day than stopping for a bit of candy on the way to school.

The little group made the four block trip to school in less than fifteen minutes. At that time Berkeley schools were neighborhood schools and just like the neighborhoods, were segregated by race. Most Negro families lived in South Berkeley where the Jameson family lived. It was one of the few areas where well-kept, affordable housing was available to Colored people. There were virtually no White residents in the South Berkeley neighborhoods.

By design, students were segregated until they got to Berkeley High School, the only public high school in town. Even then the students remained separated as a result of the 'ability tracking system' used to determine the level of classes each student should be enrolled in. Students from the predominantly Colored/Negro schools were initially systematically placed in the "slower tracks." Placements changed as students' ability dictated.

Of course there was racism in Berkeley. The city had been experiencing challenges due to its rapid growth and assimilation of its growing population. Berkeley, in the 1940's, had grown from 85,000 to 115,000. The Colored population had grown from 3,000 to 12,000 between 1940 and 1945. The majority of the White Berkeley residents did not live near or work with Colored people. Usually the only exposure White people had to Colored people was in the service industry or if they had domestic help in their homes. Sara acknowledged that even with its flaws Berkeley and the school system had been far more welcoming than Chicago, the city they had left behind. In Sara's mind there were two Berkeleys; one that had ignored the meanness that was so common in most other parts of the country and another that had grasped remnants of unfamiliar, unfriendly ways imported from other places. Reigning in her memories, remembering why she was on campus Sara found her classes, made the drive back home and had a quiet evening.

Next morning after a good night's sleep, "Opening Day" arrived and Sara moved across campus and through the hallways as if she belonged there. She felt she did. The other students were unfazed by her presence, as if they too felt she belonged. Sara got to her first class early, found her seat and opened her book. The other students began to file in followed by the instructor greeting them with a booming "Good Morning, Welcome to English 1A."

The seats on either side of Sara were filled quickly, to her left a young White woman and to her right another young White woman, each glanced at Sara and smiled. For some reason Sara felt relieved, she hadn't noticed that she was holding her breath until she silently exhaled. Everything was going to be fine.

###

Sara hadn't told anyone other than her managers at work about her plans to return to school. She was not one to be influenced or swayed by others opinions, but she was afraid that she could be distracted. Until she was sure of her footing, she would keep the news to herself.

After several weeks and as many good grades, Sara began to share her news with friends and family. Of course her children were delighted with her and for her, while the reaction from friends was mixed.

"I guess now that your children are gone it's something to do" or "Why are you doing that at this late date?" or "What good is getting a degree going to do at this point?"

Sara answered by not answering because what other people thought of her hardly mattered. Sara danced to a tune that only she heard.

Sara took to her new routine as if she was born to it. She was up and out in time for class, mixing with students and instructors with ease, developing friendships; joining study groups and generally being in the mix. She moved from school to work without breaking her stride, taking on a supervisory role on the swing shift. When things at work were slow she filled the time by completing her school assignments, finishing by the end of the shift.

Some nights after work, she and her coworkers would go for drinks at Little Esther's in downtown Oakland, closing down the club. Other nights it was home to find company, usually one of her children, Tessa, Ronald, Gregory or Patrice with at least one of their friends waiting, as her home was now the late night spot. Whatever the case, the music was always the star of the show and Sara was center stage. Sara would select a stack of LPs, long playing albums, which were good for at least four hours of listening pleasure.

Her children always brought friends who were familiar; kids who had grown up on Julia Street, Sara had known some of them since birth.

The stories from the old days were plentiful and one of the family friends would share, "At the Jameson's house there was a tug of war between watching TV and listening to Mrs. Jameson's music and stories," which the children had seemed all too happy to lose.

Sara's love of music had always been evident. She had often shared, "When I attended DuSable High School on the Southside of Chicago where I grew up, I went to school with now famous musicians like Nat King Cole and Johnny Hartman. They performed for us throughout my high school years. I fell in love with their music then and love their music still."

Sara always added to her record collection whenever she heard something new that she wanted to hear again. When the children were young Sara tended to listen to her music "serially;" she would play a song over and over until she found another to take its place. It was not uncommon for her to play only one track on an LP or only one side of a 45, ignoring the other selections. All the children had made fun of Sara's habit by saying the name of the song and exaggerating the amount of time she had played it, *"Take the A Train"*, three hours."

Whenever Sara had been ready for her next song she would send the children down to Reid's Records, a Colored-owned and operated store that had been in business since 1945 located several blocks down Sacramento Street near Alcatraz Avenue. They would pick up the latest 45 or LP for Sara's listening pleasure. Sara was generous with her music and her thoughts on music as long as the other listeners enjoyed hearing, over and over, one song at a time.

Occasionally a song managed to stay on deck even when it was no longer the favored song. Somehow a song would find its way back into the rotation like her perennial favorite "Do Nothing Till You Hear from Me" by just about anybody. Hearing the perennial favorites someone would invariably remark "that must be Sara's song."

When visiting the Jameson home the neighborhood kids had believed it was the best of both worlds when they were able to blend watching TV with listening to music; like watching the Ed Sullivan Show on Sunday nights. On those occasions Sara had shared her thoughts about guest stars like Count Basie, Louis Armstrong, Sarah Vaughn, Ella Fitzgerald and the Ink Spots.

One of the kids would ask, "Mrs. Jameson, who do you think is the better singer, Ella Fitzgerald or Sarah Vaughn?"

Sara might have replied, "That's like asking which do you need most, water or air," or she might ask, "When you go to buy a new pair of shoes are you asked "Do you want the right or the left shoe?" No, we need both. Now just listen to Sarah's voice; she is the master of embellishment. She adds flourishes were there usually are none. But Ella is the opposite, there is nothing added, her voice is pure and as clear as a bell. We need both."

And sometimes on the walk to school on the following Monday morning the children had their own discussions and had done imitations of the performers they had seen on TV the night before. Among their favorites and the funniest were their imitations of the Ink Spots singing *If I Didn't Care* along with the accompanying choreography, imitating the lead singer holding his hand up to the light so that his diamond rings sparkled as he sang.

Listening as they shared the old stories, to Sara's delight the children on Julia Street had grown up to be who the always were. Now they were just taller, wiser and old enough to drink. Sara had loved them all when they were little and she loved them now that they were adults. It had caught Sara unawares when they shared that more than anything when they were young they had loved to hear her talk, saying they loved the sound of her voice.

"Man, we knew your mom was smart, it was the confident way she said things, the way she put her words together."

"Even as kids we knew that Mrs. Jameson was an expert on everything."

They had also admired Sara's manner. Sara was calm and consistent in almost any situation; she had a standard set of go-to responses they had found comforting.

Most of all they had loved the times when Sara's friends visited and she talked about music or about her old neighborhood or going to high school in Chicago. Sara and her friends would all talk at once, not in an angry way, but in an excited way while smoking their Winston's and drinking their Cutty Sark. They would have a meal and everyone would dance until it was very late and then they would all go home or sometimes they would stay till the next day.

The memory sharing continued with how much they had enjoyed listening when the women from the neighborhood had gotten together; to do craft projects, play cards, or just chat.

The children had watched the adults over the years as they dealt with all kinds of situations. As a group, the neighborhood women had experienced extreme sadness, joy, setbacks and all had survived. The children had never seen any of the neighborhood women cry, even though tragedy had not been a stranger on Julia Street. Over the years, the neighborhood had shared the profound grief of husbands dying; one killed in an unspeakable industrial accident, mental, physical illnesses or cruel circumstances taking away the planned futures of beloved children. And still no tears were shed, at least not where kids could see them. Nor could they remember having heard any of the Julia Street women use bad language. Even as young kids they had known what bad words were, they had heard the men on Sacramento Street say them. They had also heard the men on Sacramento Street say, when a girl or woman was within earshot, "There's a lady coming by," and the bad language would stop. It seemed that bad words were more the provenance of men, not ladies.

The connection the Julia Street "kids" all felt one to another and to Sara had only deepened over the years. Now that the playing field was leveled by time and life experiences Sara was considered a friend in addition to being someone's mother. In light of this new status, details were shared that would not have been appropriate or understood before they had all walked down similar paths.

After a particularly long shift at work, one night Sara arrived home to find Ronald and Joseph, a family friend since they were in Junior High, in her living room. They both could tell at a glance that Sara's day did not go well. Not knowing if the problem was at school or at work, Ronald asked a generic "Mama, what's the matter?"

With a brusque shake of her head Sara replied while searching her handbag, "Let me read you something, 'Dear Sara Jameson, Thank you for your interest in the Freight Specialist Supervisor 2 position. We were very favorably impressed with your qualifications and although your test scores (written and oral), number of commendations, and recommendations are far superior to the other candidates, we have made the decision to select Jane Smith for the promotion'. There's more but I've read this too many times already. As you can imagine Jane Smith is not Black; that qualification seems to be the only one that I lack. On a brighter note, I got my English paper back today. I got an A and the professor's note read 'Excellent use of life experiences to bolster your points'. I guess somebody finds value in being Black." With that said, there was laughter, another cigarette, maybe a touch more Cutty Sark and music, because that's just the way it was.

Chorus:

"Nature Boy"

"Tessa who is the little dumpling holding your hand?" called Sara from the front door as she always did when she saw Tessa and her five year old son Carl headed her way. It was a typical Saturday morning and Sara was expecting at least some of her children and grandchildren to visit. As they all lived nearby and were inclined to visit, she was never sure who might show up.

"Grandma, it's me Carl" he replied with a wide grin.

"That can't be Carl, I just saw Carl the other day and he wasn't quite that tall or that handsome. Are you sure you're Carl?"

Arriving at the door, Sara's first born grandchild replied, just as he always did, "See, it's me Grandma!"

"It is you, I hardly recognized you. You get taller and more handsome every time I see you," Sara smiled as she placed his small hand in hers.

Carl stood a little straighter and smiled even brighter as he accepted praise from his grandmother as if he had never heard it before. Being the first born grandchild and the only grandson, Carl held a special place in Sara's heart. Sara has three grandchildren; Carl, Charlene, and Robin and the older Jameson girls continued to tease about boys being Sara's favorites.

Closing the door behind them, Tessa inquired, "Mama, what are you doing today?"

"Just waiting for you guys to come over. Tessa, give Carl some of the grapes from the refrigerator and pour us some coffee," Sara instructed.

Handing Carl his grapes and Sara her coffee, Tessa placed her own mug on the end table and took a seat in the chair next to the front door.

"Grandma did you buy these grapes just for me," asked Carl with a twinkle in his eye.

"Of course" replied Sara and Tessa, both chuckling.

"I noticed a moving van down the street as we were walking down Julia Street. It seems like every time we come over here somebody is moving in or out of the neighborhood. Things just aren't the same anymore since the Grabels moved away." shared Tessa wistfully.

The 1500 block of Julia Street was changing, not just in appearance, but in fact. The neighborhood felt like a puzzle whose pieces were thrown into the air and were landing in a haphazard fashion. A few of the single family homes which had been home to long-term friends and neighbors had been converted to apartment buildings. Original owners like Eva and Mrs. McArthur had moved away, replaced by strangers.

Some of the new people moving into the apartment buildings seemed to have different priorities and goals than the long-term homeowners, seeming to have a more tenuous hold on the future; their footing seemed not as firm. Their time horizon seemed shorter; needing to make it through the month, the week or the day rather than having the long view.

Before she moved, Mary and Sara talked about the changes in the neighborhood, lamenting how different everything was. They agreed that maybe it wasn't so much the people themselves that were so different, but their circumstances. They surmised that many of the new neighbors had not lived through the Great Depression, World War II, or segregation at its most prevalent, therefore, they had not developed the same coping skills that the older homeowners had been forced to develop. Most of the new neighbors did not have the benefit of their mothers living-in and managing their households while they built their careers and got a head start on adult life. By the end of their conversation Sara and Mary agreed that to a large degree circumstances had worked in their favor when they were starting out but it seemed that was no longer the case. With very little overlap in background and experience, Sara was friendly but had no friends among the new neighbors.

Sara said wistfully, "Ever since the Grabels moved the neighborhood hasn't felt the same to me either." Sara missed Mary terribly.

Sara's visits with family had an easy rhythm; their conversations moved backward to old times, on to current events, forward to include plans for the future.

"Carl is doing well in kindergarten" beamed Tessa "And I can't believe all the things they're learning. I was telling Ronald about it, he said all they did was nap and eat graham crackers when he was in kindergarten. I guess Carl's class will be doing algebra before it's all over."

Carl chimed in, "We saw grandpa on the way over here."

While Sara had taken refuge in her music and her school experiences, Ben had retreated even more into himself; becoming more of a fixture on Sacramento Street. As time passed the mainstream businesses which most people on Julia Street used regularly and the pool hall and tiny night club, which most people on Julia Street had never visited at all, seemed to battle for Sara's attention. She noticed the pool hall and tiny night club looking tired and battered, mirroring the men who stood in front of them. The buildings and the patrons were aging in place, Ben among them.

Knowing this was not an easy topic for Sara Tessa quickly changed the subject. "Mama, remember the two Japanese families who lived on the corner of Julia and California? Remember Ronald had a friend from one of the families, Jimmy Adachi. I think his son is in Carl's class."

It had been well known in the neighborhood that members of those two families had been held in a Japanese internment camp when the order for internment was given in the early 1940s. Most of those interred were second generation Japanese American citizens, born in the United States. The Northern California internees were initially gathered at processing stations located in Stockton, Fresno or Merced. From there they were often sent with just the clothes on their backs to locations with cold winters like Wyoming. The accommodations had been awful at best. Some died due to lack of medical attention and others had been killed by guards. In order to survive and make sense of their circumstances most had adopted an attitude of "shikata ga nai," which loosely translated means "It cannot be helped." In December, 1944 those with a place to return to had been released, many had lost their homes or had sold them to opportunists at next to nothing. The day they were processed out of the camp they had each been given a train ticket back to wherever they came from and twenty-five dollars cash. The Jamesons did not know very much of their Japanese neighbors' story other than the families had been taken from their homes, detained in a camp and later returned to the neighborhood.

"They were nice people, always friendly but never joined the neighborhood get-togethers. I often wonder what happened to them. Maybe through Carl and his classmate we can reconnect with the family" replied Sara in earnest. "Isn't their story something? I would love to hear about it from one of them if it isn't too painful to tell. All you have to do is knock on any door and I'm sure whoever answers has a story. Tragedy is rarely a stranger."

So the day went, just any typical Saturday. All or some combination of Sara's children and grandchildren would stay for a meal requiring a trip to Sacramento Market.

On this particular Saturday Gregory grown up and married with a daughter of his own; Charlene, made the trip.

He shared when he returned from the store "Every time I step into that store it's like stepping back into my childhood. Almost all of the same people work there and some of the same people are still shopping there. I want to say some of the same cans are still on the same shelves. And I always run into someone from the old neighborhood who wants to chat. Like today I saw Grandma's friend Miss McMurray, she still has a cigarette hanging out of the side of her mouth and her hair is still helter-skelter, after all this time she looks just like she did when I was a little boy."

Stories of Miss McMurray and their Grandma were retold including the ones featuring the women's love of horse races and the time they had spent pouring over racing forms before going to the track. They all laughed about the ladies trips to the track and to their bookie, but mostly they talked about how much they missed their grandmother, Tessa Crawford.

More serious stories were told about Mrs. Crawford's time as a domestic worker after the older Jameson children started junior high school. In order to move into the cottage behind the Jameson family home and pay her own way she had taken a job as a domestic worker for a White family in a home in the Berkeley Hills. Mrs. Crawford had a host of skills and abilities that her new employer benefitted from: she was an excellent cook, an accomplished baker, meticulous housekeeper and a talented seamstress; she baked every Monday and made all of her own clothes by hand.

In her domestic role, Mrs. Crawford's work days had started early and ended late. Monday through Friday when Sara worked day shift she and Sara had walked the few blocks together to catch their rides each morning. At that time there was only one bus in the morning at 6:20 A.M. going up Ashby Avenue into the hills and one bus coming back down Ashby to Sacramento Street arriving in the evening at 7:30 P.M. It was said that the bus service on Ashby was designed solely to get the domestic workers to their jobs in time to complete the breakfast chores in the morning and back home in the evening after the dinner chores had been done. If Mrs. Crawford was needed at work on the weekends either her employer would pick her up and take her to work or one of the Jamesons would give her a ride. There had been no bus service on the weekend going into the Berkeley Hills from Ashby Avenue and Sacramento Street.

With the stories all told, their Saturday wound down while some family members went home and others lingered past dusk. Sara enjoyed the quiet of evening, after dinner and before the rest of her family began preparing to head home. Sitting at her dining room window, Sara had been able to hear the grandchildren playing in the front yard; the sounds of their games were unmistakable and were always accompanied by laughter and the obligatory shrieking and screaming.

The night games always included the neighborhood girls singing, "Oh Mary Mack, Mack, Mack all dressed in black, black, black with silver buttons, buttons, buttons all down her back, back, back." Or "Oh little playmate come out and play with me and bring your dolly three, climb up my apple tree" when suddenly someone would scream and everyone who was within earshot knew a mistake had been made while clapping, jumping rope or singing the song. When the laughing and screaming subsided the game would start again from the beginning, "Oh Mary Mack, Mack, Mack all dressed in black, black, black."

The screaming and shrieking was also heard whenever one of the children was found in their un-findable hiding place during hide-and-seek. "How did you find me? Someone showed you where I was hiding!" they would squeal while running back to home base lest they be *it* in the next round.

There was a victorious shriek whenever someone successfully jumped from one end of the hop scotch board to the other. And so it went.

Always the first to arrive and the last to leave, Tessa said gently "Mama, we had such a good day, thank you. We better head home Carl."

"But I'm not ready," Carl whined.

"Please get ready," replied Tessa with finality.

Placing a light kiss on his forehead before they closed the door Sara whispered to Carl as she always did, "Don't be a stranger."

And as he always replied, "I won't. I want you to recnize me."

Third Verse:

"Round Midnight"

There didn't seem to be a solution, at least not one Sara could conjure up. She was losing sleep and losing focus. She went to bed early but just laid there, eyes wide open. Things that were troubling by day were far more troubling at night and problems always traveled in packs. When one problem was entertained the door was opened wide for all of the others. Things that were so right were now terribly wrong.

Adding to Sara's personal unease were the almost daily protests against the Viet Nam war or injustice in general held on Sproul Plaza, some peaceful and others not so peaceful. Protesters were routinely tear gassed or "encouraged" to move along. It was a contentious time in America, and in many cases, Berkeley and the UC campus were in the spotlight. The nation was caught up in conflict at home and internationally.

The Viet Nam War was being waged abroad while dissidents staging demonstrations across the country were demanding withdrawal from the war and long overdue freedoms. The Black Panthers with their black berets, black leather jackets and rifles were visible in neighborhoods in Berkeley and Oakland and on the nightly news.

Given Sara's job on the Base, her position on the war was complicated. The Oakland Army Base was home to the largest military port complex in the world during the Vietnam era and was called the Gateway into and out of Vietnam. Soldiers and their families relied on the personnel at the Base to provide them and their belongings safe passage and Sara felt a personal responsibility to the soldiers and their loved ones.

When soldiers arrived back at the Oakland Base for separation from the army at the end of their service they were deposited by bus in front of a building adjacent to Sara's, it was a sight that greeted her daily. The returnee area was quarantined from the area containing the replacements waiting to go to Vietnam. Most of the out-processing consisted of paperwork, a cursory physical examination, and the delivery of a new uniform for going home with a combat patch sewed on the right sleeve. Just like that, servicemen in Vietnam changed command. Operations were handled by Military Ocean Terminal Bay Area (MOTBA) where Sara worked helping to process the over 37 million tons of cargo that passed through MOTBA and its associated commercial piers during eight years of the Vietnam conflict.

Sara's feelings on the war were complicated.

In addition to the war, the 60's were moving the country away from the conservatism of the 50's. There were sweeping changes which had broad impact on everyday life and lifestyles. Education, politics, literature, personal values, housing, art and entertainment were significantly affected. These sweeping changes had a profound effect on the Black community, impacting how and where people could live, the opportunities afforded them and the resources available to be equipped to take advantage of new possibilities.

Major laws were signed in an attempt to level the playing field for all Americans. The makeup of households, neighborhoods, cities, states and the nation, if not the world, was shifting, no doubt in some ways it was the best and the worst of times. At this point, everyone was finding their way in an ever-shifting environment.

Art and architecture were changing, inspiring the viewer to take a leap into the unknown and experience art in their own way, away from the literal to a more abstract view. Architecture was taking on a more modern contemporary look. Tall buildings or skyscrapers created a distinctly American structural type, easily recognizable as an American design. Everything was new and shiny relative to other parts of the world.

Literature was forever altered by the style of writing introduced in the 1960's, reflecting the author's perceptions of what was happening in the political and social arenas of America. Race, class and sex dominated popular titles informing and to a large extent changing public opinion.

Public education was experiencing a major overhaul, teaching methods were revised with newer approaches replacing more fundamental tried and true methods. High school and college campuses were embracing debate and protest with University of California at Berkeley taking center stage nationally and internationally.

Perhaps most visible were the changes in fashion, conventional dress among men and women was replaced by blue jeans and t-shirts. Afros became the norm among Blacks while long straight hair replaced the buzz cut or bouffant hairdos worn by White men and women respectively.

Music was taking a new turn; Motown, Rhythm and Blues were at the height of popularity in Black and White communities. Radio continued to bring music into homes for listening pleasure. Television began to supplement radio allowing Black and White teens to listen to the latest music and learn the latest dances. Teens were watching American Bandstand from coast-to-coast. Literally everything was changing.

Sara's steps were becoming less firm, highlighting her personal problems. Even the drive to campus was causing Sara stress; palms sweating, making it difficult to hold onto the steering wheel, adding to her anxiety. Getting out of the car after she parked, her legs felt like lead, each step a chore. The short walk from the car to the classroom which had once been a pleasure now felt like she was headed for a date with doom.

The Statistics 101 class room was located in an area of campus that was unfamiliar to Sara, the people in the class were different than the people in her other classes, and the language spoken by the students, the instructor and written in the textbook seemed foreign.

The small slights were the hardest; the instructor refused to acknowledge her raised hand, referring to her as ma'am rather than Ms. as he did the other female students. He made her feel invisible by turning his back when she approached and conspicuous by calling on her when she was most unprepared. She felt invisible and conspicuous at the same time.

But the crushing blow landed when she got her test back and saw that he gave her an "F", the first "F" she'd gotten, ever. It was a complete bolt out of the blue. Before coming into the University Sara had tested out of a number of classes and since entering made "A"s in all of the others.

Sara's solid study habits, common sense and good instincts were not helpful in the face of a textbook filled with words that meant absolutely nothing to her. She felt like she was doing advanced study in a foreign language without having completed any of the prerequisites. She checked and rechecked the course catalog to make sure she hadn't signed up for a class that was intended for students who were majoring in Statistics or at least who had studied Statistics before. No, her class was for non-majors and it was entry level AND she needed it for graduation.

Her confidence flagging, almost daily Sara had to remind herself that she had lived through the Depression, a World War, racism and segregation at their height and a marriage that had left at least six broken hearts in its wake.

To think that Statistics 101 would be her undoing was almost laughable but she was not laughing. Quite the opposite.

Sara tried everything she could think of to get on track; she spent more time studying, re-reading her notes and the textbook. She tried studying with other people but that only made her feel more incompetent and ill prepared. She even had a few sessions with a tutor who told her he "enjoyed meeting with her and needed the money but didn't feel he could help her as she was too far behind." Sara felt helpless and alone. She was also frightened. She'd never felt so defeated. She had always been able to draw on her inner resources to "pull it off", "get it done" or at least look like she knew what she was doing. Sara was consumed by doubt and thought of little else; she agonized, prayed, lost confidence and sleep over Statistics 101.

What Sara didn't do was talk to any of her friends or family about her worries, frankly being embarrassed. Afraid they might say "I'm surprised you made it this far" or "You didn't have any plans once you got your degree anyway." Instead Sara turned inward, spending too many hours alone; she went to class, to work and then back home again to be alone. She didn't welcome company, blaming a packed schedule. Her music selections, once uplifting and fun, turned dark; Billie Holiday was her only companion. Most times there was NO music at all.

Not trusting her future, Sara longed for the familiar and took refuge in her past. Looking back instead of forward, Sara spent hours traveling down long paths, allowing her mind to take her wherever it wanted to go. She took comfort in her fondest memories.

Sara and Ben had watched their children grow in the way of all parents during that time, sort of like interested bystanders; providing direction, encouragement and course correction when needed. At that time the roles of parents and children had little overlap; each had clearly defined expectations and responsibilities. Parents went to work each day and took care of the household while children went to school and did whatever was necessary to meet the requirements set by their parents and teachers. Parents did not go to their child's school other than for evening programs or teacher's meetings, unless there was trouble. Children never went to work with their parents unless under rare and special circumstances. The lines were clearly drawn and everyone stayed on their side of the line.

Sara's children's junior high years had been a favorite time for her. She'd had confidence in their choices, allowing them to take full advantage of all of the school and social opportunities that junior high had to offer. By her children's accounts, after school, once their homework had been completed or ignored, they had lots of time to have fun. Most of their activities had revolved around school; they had attended school dances, school movies, sporting events and were entertained by students in school sponsored talent shows. At that time they were too young to own cars or have friends who owned cars so wherever they went they walked or took the bus. According to them their walks through Berkeley neighborhoods had afforded them time to think out loud, share their dreams, plans, fears and ambitions.

The stories they loved to tell were of their "free days" when there was no school. Once Sara and Mrs. Crawford left for work, their little group of friends had been in charge of themselves and their days were long, in a good way. Anxious to experience all that Berkeley had to offer, they had gotten up early, gotten themselves dressed, had breakfast and completed their chores. They met out front, made their plans and then rode their bikes, single file, down the sidewalk; they had been instructed never to ride in the street. Exploring Berkeley on foot or bicycle, according to them, the Julia Street children had felt the world was at their fingertips. They felt comfortable almost anywhere in the city, day or night. The group had often set out with no particular destination in mind and went wherever the group consensus took them.

They had never really worried about having money because Mrs. Nicholas, owner of the small market across the street on Sacramento, let them charge things, within reason, and had allowed them to pay when their parents got home from work. Tessa was in charge of paying the Jameson "bill". Sara had been aware that Mrs. Nicholas was extending her children a kindness and where some people held on to hurt Sara kept track of kindnesses and repaid them however she could.

After deciding on the meal, they would eat lunch at home or make a picnic at San Pablo Park. On very ambitious days they would walk or ride their bikes down to Aquatic Park near University Avenue to spend the afternoon just relaxing and watching the water.

When their school calendar had allowed, the days flowed one into the next and the group settled into an enjoyable rut. Their only pursuit that was out of the ordinary and had required preplanning was a trip to the Lorin Theater which had featured all the latest in teen movies. The Lorin was not very far from home, located on Adeline near Alcatraz Avenue and they were able to get there in a matter of minutes on foot.

"Free days" almost always followed the same pattern; the Julia Street kids got up early, had a full day of adventure and were tired out by the time they were called inside for the night. When they fell into bed, they looked forward to doing it all again the next day.

Sara was delighted with the people her children had become and were becoming, but if pressed Sara would grudgingly acknowledge that her children had not been perfect. Of course, over the years they had done things they shouldn't have done, gone places they did not have permission to go, had friends who were not the best choices, but they had always valued what other people, especially Sara, thought of them and remembered that their behavior was a reflection of the people who cared about them.

For the most part, their indiscretions had been minor, at least the ones Sara was aware of, and for that she was grateful. Sara couldn't help but smile as she was reminded of the time Gregory had been given money to get a haircut and spent it on other things. For the next three days while in the house, Gregory had worn a sombrero to cover up the fact that he had not had his hair cut. The other kids were in on the deception from the start and it took

Sara only a few minutes to catch on, but she had let it play out, mostly out of amusement and curiosity. This was the level of most of their infractions; not anything overly distressing and Sara appreciated that.

Sara loved their early teen years. She had particularly enjoyed the time she and her girls spent together in spite of the general belief that she favored the boys. She recalled the hours they had spent shopping for and selecting "just the right outfits" for their many social events.

According to convention at the time, the girls' outfits were always very similar, almost a uniform, as young ladies had a fairly narrow field of appropriate fashions to choose from. When deciding what to wear, they kept Sara's friend Eva's words and social norms in mind, "Remember for young women, adornment; clothing, accessories, hairstyles and make-up all have an important role, but most of all they must be appropriate. Serious times require serious adornment, fun times allow for relaxing the rules, but just a little."

Fitting for school days and sporting events, a white fitted blouse tucked into a circle skirt with saddle oxford shoes and perhaps a small matching scarf tied at the neck was the norm.

School dances required they wear a dress, nylons, "Sunday" shoes and inconspicuous but high quality jewelry.

An outfit for casual outings was usually a blouse tucked into a slim pair of capris worn with a pair of matching flats.

Hair was worn down and curled or pulled into a high ponytail, sometimes with a colorful scarf tied at the base.

Makeup was minimal or not used as a matter of course, but for a dance or special occasion a dash of powder, a dot of blusher, a dab of perfume and swipe of light lipstick filled the bill nicely.

Sara loved the simplicity and orderliness of those times.

Refrain:

"Every Time We Say Goodbye"

"I really haven't had a place here for a while. Everybody is grown up with a family of their own. I love living close to you all but it's time for a change." Mrs. Crawford's sister Ora Lee and her husband Coy had relocated to Los Angeles and suggested Tessa (Mrs. Crawford) join them promising that employment and housing opportunities were plentiful in the area near their home. Tessa Crawford had accepted their invitation.

Already unsteady, this news nearly knocked Sara off of her feet.

During the day Sara was able to see the rationale behind the move, Tessa Crawford and her sister Ora Lee delighted in each other and it seemed that Coy's only reason for being was to make sure the two sisters' relationship flourished. Sara was fine with the move during the day but once night started its descent she was sure that everything that could go wrong would go wrong. Her thoughts were on a continuous negative loop; it was too far away to visit regularly. In case of an emergency it would take too long for Sara to get there. All of her mothers' friends are here and what about Mrs. McMurray? Sara could list all of the reasons this move was not the best move. But since the move was happening, Sara prayed she was mistaken.

Within a matter of weeks, Mrs. Crawford was settled into a job and a furnished studio apartment very close to her sister's home in a cozy neighborhood, and almost as important, a five-minute walk to her new bookie. Mrs. Crawford was happy with her studio and happily employed. Sara spoke to her mother regularly via telephone catching up on each other's news. At the end of each conversation Mrs. Crawford added "well now we know everything" just before hanging up. Hearing the contentment in her mother's voice, Sara and family were happy for her. While they were happy that she was happy, Sara missed her terribly.

At about the same time, Sara wondered what brought Ben back to the house on Julia Street on such a regular basis. Their children were grown up and he no longer lived there, but Ben decided that it was time to build the second floor bathroom. He bought the materials on his own and did most of the work in the evenings, on the weekends or days when he didn't have a paying job. Some days when Sara got home from class or work, there he'd be. As there was no set deadline, it seemed like a never ending project, a way to legitimize the amount of time he spent at the house on Julia Street.

One positive effect of having Ben working on the house was that he and their grandson Carl were becoming constant companions. One beautiful Sunday afternoon Ben and Carl were planning to take a ride through Berkeley so that Ben could show Carl some of the projects he had worked on over the years. Ben had continued to build his skills as a carpenter and was eager to show them off and he asked Sara to join them. She agreed as she wanted to point out Berkeley High School (again) and U.C. Berkeley (again) to Carl.

As Ben slowly backed out of the driveway, continued down Julia Street then turned right onto Sacramento, Sara noticed the men standing in front of the liquor store and tiny night club as usual. She thought of the last trip she and Carl made to the market, he had been quite intent on getting answers to his questions as they crossed Sacramento Street. He asked about the group of men standing idly on the street.

"Why are they just standing there all the time?"
"Do they have families?"
"Do they have jobs?"
"Are they unhappy?"
"Will they stand there forever?" Carl asked.

Sara didn't give much explanation; she was smart enough to know the concern Carl had about the situation on Sacramento Street was as a result of having seen his grandpa standing in the crowd.

Sara always spoke to Carl as if he was fully able to understand her and most times he did. When he didn't understand he asked more questions.

"I'm sure most of them have families and at one

time I'm sure they had jobs or may still have jobs, responded Sara. They may have suffered disappointments that they have yet to recover from. Hold a good thought for them. Where there's life, there's hope."

After riding in silence for a few blocks Carl exclaimed from the back seat pointing excitedly, "There's my school! Grandma, remember where you pick me up sometimes? There's the gate right there, we go in that gate every morning too!"

Sara had no problem visualizing Carl running through the gate each school day just in time to line up with his class after making a short stop at the little corner grocery store right across the street on Ward and California Streets. Like most of the children he would take his place with the other kids who were lined up to go into the store to buy their supply of penny candy for the day. The store owner would allow two kids to go in at a time, rushing them to get their transactions done so that the next set of kids could go in. With years of practice, without fail, the owner moved the line along in time to get all of the kids in and out before the first bell rang.

"Yes, I remember. That's where you meet me, right there," replied Sara as she pointed from the front passenger window. Sara thought of the first time she picked up Carl after school. She had been struck by what a difference almost twenty years had made, since her children had gone to elementary school. For the most part gone were the crisp cotton pastel dresses with matching cardigans worn with the saddle oxford shoes and the neat rows of plaits most of the girls had worn. On this day Sara was saddened to see three girls, who must have been under the age of ten, wearing black leather jackets and black leather high heeled knee high boots and very grown up looking hairstyles. Sara was certain that wearing those boots would put those three girls on a path most of the Longfellow students would never travel. Sara silently wished them well.

"Grandma, is that your school?!" cried Carl.

Sara, lost in her thoughts had not noticed the route they were traveling. "No, that's Berkeley High, remember? The high school that your mother, aunt, and uncles went to when they were teenagers."

"When were they teenagers?" Carl asked with a note of skepticism in his voice.

"Not that long ago, they grew up, just like you're doing. Every year they're another year older just like you are." replied Ben with a smile.

"Carl, we're not that far from my school. Look for the people selling things on the sidewalks and then start looking for the archway at my school," advised Sara.

"There it is, I see the people selling stuff and I see your school Grandma. It's big, I like your school." shared Carl his face pressed against the window.

"I'm glad you like it. I like it too, maybe someday you'll go here too," expressed Sara.

"Will you still be going here when I go here?" asked Carl hopefully.

Both Ben and Sara laughed when Sara replied, "Oh, I hope not."

Driving away from campus and into the Berkeley Hills Ben pointed out projects he had completed. He was proud of his accomplishments and Carl seemed very proud as well. Ben enjoyed being able to point out the physical fruits of his labor but not all of Ben's experiences in the Berkeley Hills had been positive.

As Carl began to doze, Ben shared with Sara "I can't count the number of times I have been pulled over by the police on my way to and from work, the officers always inquiring why I'm in this part of town. I explain that I'm a carpenter working in the area. Most times the officer has asked for the address of the project, looked in the back seat of the car at my tools and sent me on my way. It's not as bad now but I always leave a little extra time in my commute to allow for being stopped. That way I'm not late."

Noting the beauty of the surroundings, the large meticulously groomed front yards with majestic trees scanning both sides of the street, with a slight sadness Sara asked Ben "Are there any Black families living in these neighborhoods?"

Taking a moment to think Ben replied, "Not many that I've seen." He explained that most likely the cause was the 'gentleman's agreement' from the 1940's and 50's not to sell property to Colored people north of Grove Street which created the almost all White neighborhoods in the Berkeley Hills. In those days to secure property in a "restricted area" a Colored family had to get a White person to "front for them." In most cases the sale would be too far along to cancel when the agent discovered the buyer was Colored.

As they rode in silence Sara looked over at Ben and saw traces of why she had married him. Even when love's gone it lingers. Ben was still quite good looking and his intelligence was still attractive. He was a man of few words but he chose them carefully, his meaning always clear. There had been good times in their marriage; among them were the weeks in the boarding house, the social club dances and the friends they had in common and the moments Ben shared with Tessa and Patrice as little girls. Sara recalled the times Tessa, reading a book, sat at Ben's feet while he stroked her hair as he read the newspaper. She was reminded of Patrice following Ben upstairs when he came home unexpectedly and how he had been so glad to see her there. Sara saw much of the same gentleness when Ben interacted with Carl.

Interrupting Sara's thoughts, Ben casually shared that the job opportunities he had been accustomed to were becoming fewer and far between. Berkeley was shifting from a town with an abundance of "blue collar" opportunities to an intellectual town catering to white collar industries. Ben was able to find work but not with the ease of the early years when building was booming. Berkeley continued to lose dozens of manufacturing plants along the West Berkeley Industrial Core. The decline in "smoke stack" industries was a nation-wide phenomenon which had impact on the building industry and a disproportionately negative impact on Blacks. Technological developments were causing major changes. The job market continued to shift from blue-collar jobs to white-collar careers.

In response to Ben's concerns Sara casually shared her difficulties with Statistics 101 and her mixed feelings about her mother's move. While neither had answers for the other, they shared a belief that things would work out.

"Don't Go To Strangers"

Her footsteps echoing off of the hardwood as she moved through her small dining alcove, Sara reached down and turned on the console radio tuning in KJAZ, her favorite station. Again she called on music and again it didn't fail her. After a short while, making a spur of the moment decision to leave rather than stay and stew; Sara grabbed her purse, flung her shawl over her shoulders and headed for the door.

Making a right turn at Sacramento Street and a U-turn at Russell, Sara was going to visit Ken and Hazel. She had her window rolled down, her radio turned up, and a cigarette burning in the ashtray. Driving across the Bay Bridge well after dusk, headed toward the city was one of Sara's favorite things to do.

The Harrisons lived in San Francisco in a housing project which had initially been built for shipyard workers employed at Hunter's Point. The buildings were remote, somewhat desolate and made entirely of concrete and glass. The Harrison's unit had outside access and was on the ground level. Outside of their living room and kitchen windows were a few patches of brown grass which the Harrison family kept free of debris. Most of the outdoor space was covered in cement and gravel with almost no area in which to play.

The inside of the Harrison's home was compact, a small living room, two small bedrooms, one small bath, and a tiny kitchen. Their home was always spotless and very homey. Mrs. Harrison was a homemaker, a seamstress, an excellent cook and an extraordinarily kind woman who seemed to spend all of her time taking care of others. Ken Harrison was one of the few thousand workers that had been retained at the Richmond Shipyards after the war ended. When he was not working, Ken was an accomplished artist, something he and Sara's son Gregory had in common. Looking around their home at Ken's finished pieces it was obvious that he was comfortable working in clay, oils, colored pencil and graphite.

As Hazel hugged her "hello" Sara set down her bag and shawl, taking what had become "her" chair. Feeling no need to apologize for not calling first as it was customary for Sara to just appear at their door and the same was true for them at Sara's house.

Hazel welcomed Sara by asking "How was the drive?"

"Hardly any traffic at all, just me, a few truck drivers and a beautiful view of the bay and the skyline," shared Sara.

Ken appeared with a glass in hand which Sara accepted with a smile.

Sara felt at home at the Harrisons anytime. After dark the coffee turned to Cutty Sark and the conversation became more spirited, mostly revolving around the music. They listened to the latest and the favorites by Thelonious Monk, Jon Hendricks and Miles Davis. Debated who is the best artist, what is the best rendition and who they were planning to see perform live in the coming months. Questions were asked and answered about the arrangements for the Monterey Jazz Festival in September. They routinely argued and planned.

Their group (not Ben, but including all of their children) had been making the trip down to the Monterey Jazz Festival since its inception in September of 1958. The line-up at the first festival had been stellar according to Sara. Performers had included Billie Holliday in one of her final performances; she died just nine months later. Dizzy Gillespie, Louis Armstrong, and Dave Brubeck were among many others. The quality of the performances had remained high in the subsequent years.

They always left on Friday afternoon after school and stayed until Sunday night. They always had three adjacent rooms but not adjoining, maintaining the function of each room and some sense of privacy.

One room was set up with a record player and LPs. The collection included albums from current and past Jazz Festival performers. The middle room was filled with food, cooked, uncooked, homemade, store bought, fresh produce, coffee and non-alcoholic drinks. The third room was converted into a bar, each flat surface laden with drinks. Ice buckets were collected from the other rooms and all three were filled and refilled throughout the weekend. Those under twenty-one were welcomed in the food and music rooms, not so much in the drinks room, where cards and the "dozens" were played.

And when they slept, they slept in these rooms too, in the beds, on the floor, in the chairs. Just a place to rest their eyes, shower, refuel and recharge.

"Did you get your confirmation from the motel?" asked Hazel.

"I got the latest from Sarah Vaughn to add to the LPs I'm bringing" said Sara.

"I hope it's not as hot as it was last year, you know September in Monterey is tricky. It can be hot as blazes or so overcast you need a coat and gloves" rejoined Ken.

The weekend always started on Friday night, went through Saturday afternoon into the late night and Sunday afternoon into the late evening. The atmosphere during the festival was like a county fair, but with good live music and no livestock. There were vendors selling LPs, food, drinks, jewelry, clothing, and just about anything you could want or imagine.

There were always two things you could count on over the weekend; great music on stage and drama in the audience. The regulars sat in the same sections in virtually the same seats every year and it was obvious whenever someone was there with someone they shouldn't have been or doing something they shouldn't have been doing.

"Did you see Babe with Stella's husband? Do they really think nobody is going to tell her they were here and in matching outfits no less?"

"Sam is drinking more than usual and that's saying something."

"Sandra needs to just go somewhere and sit down, ain't nobody buying what she's selling."

Invariably somebody thought they should sing along with the featured singer or dance in front of their chair blocking the view of the stage. Typical good natured comments expressing displeasure could include:

"Who's that on stage singing? Not you."

"I paid to see Duke Ellington and his orchestra. Are you in his orchestra?"

"I can't see through you or around you."

All this often resulted in the possibility of somebody being cussed out. Good times.

When the topic of the Festival was exhausted and the music moved into the background, as usual the conversation got around to their children, the subject they all held dear.

"How are your boys?" asked Sara with sincere interest. The Harrisons had three sons about the same age as Sara's three oldest children.

"All's well as far as I know" replied Hazel. "You know how it is with men; you can never get any real information out of them. If I didn't talk to their wives regularly I would find out I was having a new grandchild when they showed up with a baby in their arms."

Sara smiled but couldn't really relate as her children and grandchildren lived within blocks of her home and they talked and visited regularly. When asked about her family she shared the latest and the greatest, thankful that in this case no news was good news.

The shift was subtle, marked by a casual comment, allowing the masks and armor they wore daily for their protection to be peeled away.

"Remember the time Gregory brought that White girl home? Not just a White girl, but a blue-eyed blonde White girl?" Ken said with a shake of his head.

One afternoon late in the school year Gregory, about age sixteen, had brought home a classmate for a visit who happened to be a blue-eyed blonde White girl.

"I can only imagine what either of them felt when that cop pulled over to question them and then for him to FOLLOW them!" he continued.

As Gregory and his classmate were walking through South Berkeley, an all Negro neighborhood, a policeman stopped them and asked the young lady if everything was all right. She had been visibly frightened by being stopped by the police and by the questions, but she had replied that everything was fine and she was going for a visit at her friend's house. In spite of her answer the policeman had been reluctant to take her at her word and continued to follow them in his police car until they had arrived at Gregory's home and had gone inside.

Even after all this time Sara's anguish was apparent, "I remember looking at them, my son and that young girl, thinking this shouldn't be a big deal but it was. There was too much at stake, too much could change in the blink of an eye based on someone's perception."

Throughout the visit, Sara had imagined all of the things that could go wrong, realizing the young woman would survive, while her son would suffer the consequences. The visit had been pleasant enough, she had even offered to take the girl home but Gregory insisted he would walk her home.

"I waited for Gregory to get back, hoping they didn't run into anymore trouble. When he finally got home I told him 'You know you can't bring that girl back to this neighborhood.' Gregory had simply replied 'I know'," Sara said sadly.

Of course the Harrison's recounted their stories but Sara sought solace for herself.

"There are so many different ways to kill a person's spirit," continued Sara. "Like the time when Ronald had taken the test for a job at the Post Office just before graduation in order to pay for his college expenses. He was notified that he had passed and was told to report for the next step in the process. I remember him eagerly getting ready early so that he would arrive at the office in downtown Berkeley before the appointed time. He was early, found the right room and gave the attendant, who was White, his name. Ronald said the attendant began searching the list. Turns out, the list was not in alphabetical order, but in the order of highest test score at the top and lowest test scores at the bottom. The attendant had begun his search half way down the list and went down to the bottom. Ronald said he did this several times, reporting he was not able to find Ronald's name on the list. Ronald asked if he might try to find it and the attendant said, "Sure." Ronald immediately found his name. His was the first name at the top of the list - he had made the highest score on the test. Of course the implications of the attendant's actions were not lost on Ronald but I'm hopeful."

Sara's thoughts collided as she moved on to her next story which like the others had been told many times before.

"I never knew about this until many years later, I'm grateful for that at least. One afternoon on a day when school was not in session the two Gregorys, you know the other Gregory who lives across the street from us with his mother and his brother also named Ronald, well the boys took a trip to San Francisco Play Land. I think it was a school holiday but not a work holiday. The boys caught the bus over and they had a great day walking on the beach, riding all the rides, and playing in the arcades. As a prize for winning one of the games, one of them won a plastic pistol and they spent the afternoon walking around the boardwalk pulling pranks on each other using their new toy. I can see them now, they were such big kids at heart and so fun loving. Well, apparently all the fun stopped when they were accosted by Boardwalk security and turned over to the police for "brandishing a firearm." They were taken to a police substation on Treasure Island where they were detained and questioned. After several hours they were released when my Gregory's friend and her older sister came over and convinced the officers to let them go. Thank goodness the teens and their older friend were able to convince the officers that they had no "malicious intent."

This was the kind of information that had never reached Sara's ear years earlier and allowed her to believe that her children had never gotten into any serious trouble. She surmised it was likely these kinds of situations that had allowed the teens to develop the ability to solve their problems without involving adults, although it must have been disheartening. The need to continually prove you belong wherever you're standing takes a toll.

After midnight all their stories had been told for the night; most without happy endings. The masks and armor were again firmly in place until the next time. Sara bid her friends goodnight and good fortune because that's just how it was.

Fourth Verse:

"Joy Comes In the Morning"

Sara woke up counting her blessings and knowing exactly what to do. It had been one of those sleeps that brought more answers than questions. She had gone to bed early and gone right to sleep. Her slumber had been filled with images which upon waking were nothing more than impressions that left a sense of finality, as if there were only one possible plan.

Sara selected her clothes for the day, dressed quickly not even slowing down for her customary cigarette and cup of black coffee. All set, she opened and closed the front door not bothering to lock it. The Jamesons (and most other Julia Street residents) never locked their doors; she didn't even have the key anymore. For years the family had taken trips to Monterey, Los Angeles and once across country, never locking their doors and never worrying about the contents of their home. The men who stood guard on Sacramento Street were a deterrent to any and all crime and wrong doing on Julia Street. Pulling out of the driveway Sara thought, not for the first time, that thanks to the watchful eyes on Sacramento Street she had always felt safe in her neighborhood and knew in an emergency there would be many who would come to her aid. She felt it was the only upside to Ben's affiliation on Sacramento Street.

Sara made the twenty minute drive without incident and without paying much attention, having made the trip so often she was almost on autopilot. Once situated, she quickly found a convenient parking space and took the most direct footpath. Relieved to find there was no line, she was in and out in less than ten minutes. Sara rarely second-guessed herself, in this case she was quite confident in her decision saying quietly "that's done" as she walked down the short flight of stairs. "All's well that ENDs".

Headed to the Bear's Lair for a celebratory cup of coffee Sara noticed her steps were lighter and her outlook much brighter. Easily finding a seat by the window, she took a look at the form she had hastily shoved into her bag. In bold red letters the word "Dropped" was stamped across Statistics 101 on her class list. Emboldened by her actions she decided to add a celebratory patty melt to her celebratory cup of coffee.

Sara felt free. All's well that ends.

Since her schedule was freed up she took a leisurely walk around campus, something she loved but was never able to do as she was always on her way to class, in class, or leaving class on her way to work. With fresh eyes she was impressed anew by the beauty of the campus; it was lush, green and meticulously kept, clearly a place where the wealthy sent their children to be educated.

Sometime later, Sara found herself at the bookstore, one of her favorite places on campus. Instead of asking the clerk for directions she wandered down each aisle with no particular goal in mind. Serendipitously finding "The Spook Who Sat by the Door," a book that she wanted to read but never had the time before. Sara took a copy to the cashier delighted by the change to her schedule. At the head of the line just as the cashier asked "Is that all for you today?" Sara noticed the Summer/Fall Course Catalog and added it to her purchase. She paid the young woman, acknowledged her greeting of "Have a nice day" and made her way out of the store into the cool sunshine, the climate perfectly matching her mood.

"All's well that ends" thought Sara as she took just a minute to sit on a bench outside of the bookstore, leafing first through her new novel then the Course Catalog. That's when she saw it; Statistics 101, only one section was being offered during summer session and it was being taught by the instructor whose class she had just dropped.

"Good grief" exclaimed Sara while furiously flipping pages until she found the Fall entries and there it was, two sections one on Monday, Wednesday and Friday and the other on Tuesday and Thursday, both taught by the instructor she just dropped.

Sara could have easily turned morose but having just been down that path and not liking it, she decided she needed a more philosophical approach. She just needed a minute to decide which approach to take. Searching her mental files she found a much too appropriate quote "life is not just one thing after another but one thing over and over until it is resolved." Sara silently accepted the challenge of resolving this "one thing".

Arriving home with time to spare before the start of her shift at the Base, Sara took her tote bag and purchases inside and set out to do something she couldn't remember ever doing before. She began walking from the 1500 block to 1600 block of Julia Street to visit Leona. She had always made the trip by car.

Reminded of the conversations she had with her children whenever they had asked to visit someone in the next block, she remembered she had invariably said "No". Before Tessa, Ronald, Gregory or Patrice had attempted to travel from one block to the next there had always been an inquisition. It was as if California Street, the sleepy two lane road which intersected Julia, was the Himalayas. Sara chuckled at the memory.

She had invariably asked:

"Who are you going to visit down there?"

"Why are you going down there?"

"Who else is going down there with you?"

The inquisition usually ended with Sara saying, "We don't really know any of the people down there." Then she would remind them that their friends were more than welcome to visit in their home and to avoid further discussion and questioning the Jameson children had confined most of their activities to the 1500 block of Julia Street or at least the ones she was aware of.

Sara smiled as she remembered those days and wondered why she had dug in her heels on that topic; even now she had no answer.

As she crossed California Street she noticed the

YMCA and fondly recalled the number of hours her children had spent there. When they were given permission to go, their little group had walked to the neighborhood YMCA located two blocks away from home at the corners of Russell and California Streets. The building was a rather modern design made mostly of grey concrete boasting three large windows along the front façade. The interior of the building was deceptively large, full of nooks and crannies. The playground was not visible from the street, affording a higher comfort level for parents. The staff at the Y was a combination of professionals with college degrees in early childhood development and students that were still completing their studies. The staff members had interacted with the children with kindness and competence, seemingly resolving any potential issues before they developed. Sara and the other neighborhood parents had felt comfortable sending their children to the YMCA.

Continuing her short walk down both blocks of Julia Street she made a promise to leave her car at home in the future when visiting Leona unless she was picking her up for an outing. She arrived at Leona's door unannounced which was not unusual for either of them but when Leona opened the door Sara sensed immediately that something was off. Of course Leona was happy to see her that much was obvious, but Leona didn't seem quite herself.

"Hey Sara, what are you up to?" inquired Leona finding her footing before Sara could inquire about her concern.

"Nothing much, just decided to take a walk down to your neck of the woods" replied Sara trying to sound nonchalant.

"*A walk*" cried Leona. "You *walked* down here, what's gotten into you, is your car broken?"

"Nothing's gotten into me, my car is not broken. I just felt like walking, you know I love to walk." replied Sara with a bit of an attitude. "Are you going to let me in?"

"Oh, come on in. I know you love to walk but a far as I know you never do it. Now I'm a little off kilter because of the *walk*" said Leona with her signature smile.

"Well, enough about how I got here, let's talk about why I'm here" Sara rejoined.

"Have a seat while I get the coffee" said Leona as she headed toward the kitchen.

Sara took a seat next to the window accepting her coffee cup as she began sharing her story, the whole story leaving nothing out. Sara shared her feelings about her mother's move, her feelings about Statistics and the instructor, the action she had just taken and the bombshell about the Summer/Fall Statistics classes.

"Let me make sure I understand" said Leona. "The class you just dropped, mainly because of the instructor, is only being offered by that same instructor during the summer and fall?" asked Leona with incredulity.

"That's it" replied Sara. "The sections taught by other instructors are only offered while I'm at work."

"Good grief, so what are you going to do? You need that class to graduate!" said Leona preaching to the choir.

"That's why I'm here" announced Sara.

"Girl, you know I don't know nothin' about Statistics", exclaimed Leona.

"I know, and at this point neither do I but that's about to change", replied Sara firmly.

"Ok, what's the plan?" asked Leona with interest.

"First you're going to take me to Kramer" said Sara excitedly.

"Happy to do it but what does getting your hair done have to do with passing a class?" asked Leona with more than a hint of skepticism.

"I'm not just getting my hair done, I'm changing my look and outlook!" shared Sara.

"Hallelujah" praised Leona. "I've known you for over a quarter of a century and you've always worn some variation of that same hairstyle! It's about time."

"Wait just a minute. My mother always says "If you're beautiful, it doesn't matter how you wear your hair."

"Well, if we're just quoting folks, my hairdresser says "It's imperative that you know what your best look is, just don't wear it every day."

"You think I've worn my best look every day?"

"Just for twenty five years" joked Leona. "Seriously, what's going on?"

"All kidding aside" said Sara "Sometime you have to change your outside to let people know that you're different inside. I have to help my instructor see me in a different light. I'm going to make it easy for him, not just by acting different but looking different too! And that's where Kramer comes in, I'm getting an Afro."

Leona had been wearing an Afro for the past year and Sara thought her hair always looked lovely. She had been secretly craving the style for herself but didn't have the nerve to make the change. Well, desperate times call for desperate measures.

"I'm going to call right now and make the appointment for as soon as he can take you before you change your mind" said Leona reaching for the telephone.

"Not a chance. I have some other changes up my sleeve as well," replied Sara with a smile.

That all settled, Sara promised to be in front of Leona's house at 10:45 am for the 11:00 am appointment at Kramer's the following Saturday.

Saturday couldn't come fast enough for Sara. She arrived at Leona's promptly at 10:45 am, honked her horn once and waited a bit impatiently until she opened her door. Sara was as excited as she had been all those years ago when she and Mary Grabel had a girl's day of shopping. She was pleasantly surprised by the memory. As Sara remembered they had started their day in downtown Berkeley at Hink's, took the trolley into downtown Oakland spending most of their time at IMagnin and Goldman's, two very luxurious stores. In recent years downtown Oakland had lost most of its luster replaced by the convenience of El Cerrito Plaza and Richmond's Hilltop Mall.

"Well, I see you haven't chickened out" said Leona as she slid into the passenger seat. Again Sara noticed that Leona was not as bubbly as usual and this time she asked about it.

"No, I have not chickened out; I'm really excited about making this change. By the way, speaking of change, I'm noticing that you've been a little subdued the last couple times we've gotten together. Is something the matter?" asked Sara with genuine concern.

"Just trying to make sense of some things I'm not quite ready to talk about yet." Adeptly changing the subject Leona commented "I see you have on one of your new tops, kind of like a dashiki. I love the batik print. That top should really complement your new hairstyle."

Kramer's Hair Salon seemed to be the place to be, especially on a Saturday morning. Once they had been checked in by the receptionist they were seated in an area that had a full view of the action in back. Sara was impressed by the size of the shop, the opulence and the array of women receiving services. The color scheme was dominated by Black and Gold. The shampoo bowls gleamed in polished black perfectly complimented by ornate oversized gold mirrors. The chairs at each station were black leather. Kramer's was nothing like the sedate shop that Sara usually frequented.

There were all manner of women-- flashy, fancy, what they used to call "fast", plain, classy, pretty, beautiful, fat, thin, young and old. Sara watched with interest as the women were given wash and sets, press and curls, perms and afros. She also noticed that eyebrows were attended to by a woman who seemed to have a steady hand and a trained eye. She was reminded of one of Eva's favorite sayings; "Remember eyebrows are sisters not twins, they will never look exactly the same." It was her standard admonition not to try to make them match, asserting it would only end badly.

Sara loved watching the transformations. They were a very diverse group of women but what they all had in common when they were done was they were current.

They made her feel not just like a woman of a "certain age" but of a "certain era." She hoped that would change.

After the introductions and a few clarifying questions, Kramer brought Sara up to date with a wash, a small drop of hair product and a few snips of his scissors. When she looked in the mirror she looked not just good but authentic, like the best version of her current self. She then reached in her handbag, pulled out the African themed carved wooden earrings and coordinating necklace that Ken Harrison had made for her, but she had never felt comfortable wearing before, now they fit.

Back at Leona's home Leona looked over and said with a smile "Sara, go on and pass that Statistics class" just as she got out of the car.

Sara arrived early, walked up to the professor, extended her hand and said with confidence, "Good morning, I'm sure you remember me from last quarter. I'm Sara Jameson but please call me Sara. I had some difficulty during the spring session and dropped your class, but that was then. I don't intend to become a statistician but I do intend to do well in this class with your help should I need it."

Before the instructor could respond Sara took a seat directly in front of the podium in the front row and opened her textbook.

Sara had no further difficulty with Statistics; she finished the six week summer course with higher than a passing grade.

Sara had worked hard; the class had required a lot of her time and attention. In her limited free hours she built new friendships with instructors and other students. A new world opened to her, one she relished. She went to lectures, galleries, poetry readings and parties. Sara loved academia and she was in her element. All these new activities along with the time she spent with her family left little time for Sara's long time friends.

Summer had gone quickly and when Sara opened the envelope confirming her success in Statistics she decided to walk down to Leona's to catch-up and to share her good news. She hadn't seen her good friend all summer and she missed her. She looked forward to resuming their routine of impromptu visits with a cup of coffee and a chat.

As Sara walked past the single family homes still remaining in the 1500 block of Julia Street and the ones that had been converted into multifamily dwellings, she remembered the families that had moved away. She thought of Mary who was Sara's first friend on Julia Street and was still her friend. While she didn't see Mary as often as she would have liked she kept up with her through her daughters Jeannette and Nora. Sara thought of her friend Eva who had been her first hair dresser and beauty consultant in Berkeley. There was Mrs. Simpson who had passed away years ago, who had lived a few doors down but had never really been a friend. And Mrs. Mc Arthur who had been friendly but had moved away before a friendship could take root. Although Sara had lost track of many of the old neighbors she continued to hold a fondness for them.

Refrain:

"I'll be Seeing You"

When Leona's daughter opened the door at Leona's small duplex, Sara knew immediately that something was very wrong. She braced herself for bad news.

"What's wrong Janet?" asked Sara gently.

"It's mama; she wants to tell people herself." replied Janet just above a whisper.

Moving across the small living room over to where Leona was lying on the sofa, Sara was struck by how she looked. Leona's color was ashen, the whites of her eyes were yellowed and her skin seemed to hang on her small frame. In horror Sara thought to herself, I just saw you weeks ago before my class started, when you took me to have my hair done at Kramer's shop, what could have happened between then and now?

Sara took Leona's hand and said simply, "Leona?" allowing the one word to ask the questions.

"Cancer, it's untreatable. By the time it was diagnosed it was already too late." answered Leona; her voice strong despite her appearance.

"I stayed away too long, I'm sorry," Sara's response fading into the background.

"No need to be sorry, did you pass your class?" asked Leona with genuine interest.

"Yes, I came down to tell you." Sara said with sadness.

"You showed him." Leona smiled.

Sara visited daily, after class on her way to work, leaving the weekends for private family time between Leona and her girls. Sara and Leona spent most of their time together talking about the old days. How they had clicked the first time they met, their days at the boarding house and at the Richmond Shipyards.

"Can you believe how mean they were to us at the Shipyards? Being Black or Colored as we were called then, and a woman, was enough to cause them big problems. Those men ended up not knowing what to do with themselves but we didn't let it affect us" said Leona with obvious effort. "Mrs. Knight was so kind to us and her home was such a welcoming beacon in what were dark times in the country and in the world."

Sara replied "We are so fortunate to have kept our friendship all these years, it's so important to have someone in your life who knew you when."

The past takes on much more importance when it is certain there will be no future. Over the weeks Sara attended Leona on her journey and thought of her own; secretly wondering if the best days were in the past.

Several good friends had left the fold, Mary had moved away and Leona was going away. Sara wondered how twenty plus years of memories could be packed and neatly put away.

The service was held on a Thursday morning during the early fall.

"We should go Mama; we don't want to be late." Patrice suggested gently.

Stepping onto the front porch Sara felt assaulted by the sunshine. The day was crisp and cool but very clear and bright, so bright it seemed inappropriate. Just as they were about to get into the car Ben pulled into the driveway behind them. He got out of his car dressed for the occasion. He held one single yellow rose (Sara's favorite) with the small stem wound in yellow ribbon. Without a word he handed it to Patrice who pinned it to Sara's wrap.

"I'll drive." he said.

Sara was not familiar with death; no one close to her had died. Both of her parents were alive and she had never met any of her grandparents, they had died before she was born. She was finding the hardest part of death is the finality of it; Leona had been there one minute and not the next. No longer available to share good or bad news, no longer to smile that show stopper smile, no longer giving Sara a reason to walk from the 1500 to 1600 block of Julia Street.

Sara mourned her friend and the lost opportunities.

The service was held graveside. Leona had been cremated per her wishes and the scripture readings were brief. "The girls" as Leona always called them, hosted a small repast at Leona's duplex which Sara, Ben, and Patrice attended.

"The service was lovely, exactly what your mother would have wanted," said Leona as they were leaving. It was cliché but it was the truth. "I'll see you Saturday morning."

On Saturday Sara woke early, dressed for the day and made a pot of coffee. As she took her cup into the living room, the tears falling, uninvited. She cried for all of the cups of coffee she and Leona shared, the endless words of encouragement they spoke one to the other, the instant bond of friendship they felt on their first meeting and she cried for the finality of death.

Sara cried for everything she and Leona shared but she wept for everything Leona's grandchildren would never know. They would never know the wisdom of Leona's words, the strength of her convictions, and the gentleness of her admonitions.

Sara sat and cried.

Pulling herself together Sara took what she was certain would be her last walk down Julia Street to help Leona's girls empty the duplex. Crossing the threshold the absence of Leona made the space feel anonymous; there were just things where there once was a life.

As they worked they spoke of Leona, they laughed at her quirks and cried at everything.

"Don't ever stop talking about your mother; there are so many things worth sharing. Say the things she always said, the way that she said them. Tell your children what mattered to her, tell them what delighted her, perplexed her, and angered her. Show them pictures of her, as many as you can find in as many settings as possible," Sara said to the girls. "Make her a part of your children's lives."

Sara and the girls placed items into three piles; keep (which they packed as they went along), donate, and toss. Janet made several trips to Good Will donating items as quickly as her car filled up. The items to be tossed were placed in a dumpster they had rented for the day. As they neared the end of their task Janet asked Sara if there was anything she wanted to remember Leona by. Sara asked for the mug that Leona used for her coffee whenever she came for a visit.

Although Sara issued an open invitation to visit her home in the 1500 block of Julia Street, she bid them good fortune and goodbye, certain she would never see them again.

It was no surprise that Sara felt adrift; so many of her touchstones were missing. Leona, Mary, her mother, even her children and Ben were no longer within arm's reach. Sara wondered at the many changes that had occurred in her lifetime; some had been good and some, it was still too soon to tell. By far the most jarring was Leona's death, though Sara was deeply saddened, she was determined not to *be* sad, mostly because it was not her nature nor would Leona want her to be. Sara searched for answers or at least solace in scripture, literature, conversation and hours of solitude. At last she found comfort in something she read for the first time in years; "The past is never dead. It's not even past."

Heartened by a new outlook and a new day, Sara finished her coffee which she always drank from the mug Leona's daughters had given her. Without a real plan, she put down her cup and made her way into the bedroom. Her bedroom was no longer the room upstairs with the large picture window and the small balcony she had shared with Ben, it was now located on the first floor next to the only finished bathroom in the house.

In her small closet Sara found her dashiki tops, folded them then went to the dresser for the African earrings and necklace. She bundled the jewelry together with the tops and packed them into an unused dresser drawer.

Making her way back in the living room Sara could hear the street noise, children calling to one another and cars leisurely passing by as she reached for the telephone to make a call. She waited to hear the voice of her beautician, Anne to schedule an appointment for the next day.

Sara knew after Leona's death she would not go back to Kramer's salon; the whole experience and the need for her new look had died with Leona and completing the Statistics class. In her heart Sara felt she had only fit in at Kramer's when she had an agenda, something to prove. To Sara the women at Kramer's salon were 'destination women'; women who had places to go, who wanted to see and be seen. Sara knew she was not a 'destination woman'. Sara was already where she was going.

Next morning Sara dressed carefully for her hair appointment, making sure her clothing set the tone for the hairstyle she would choose. Leaving the house she allowed herself a few extra minutes not knowing the traffic obstacles she might face between home and the salon on Solano Avenue in Albany.

"Sara, so glad to see you," beamed Anne, Sara's beautician. "I love your haircut. Are you looking for a change?"

"Anne, it's good to see you too," replied Sara. "I enjoyed wearing this style but it no longer suits me. I'd really like to marry my old look with this one, sort of a combination of the two."

"We can do that," said Anne with enthusiasm. "Let's do a short hair cut and highlight your grey."

"Sounds good" Sara replied, confident in Anne's skill.

An hour later looking in the mirror from all angles Sara smiled. "I love it Anne, it's exactly right. Thank you."

Back at home it all started innocently enough, just doing chores but before it was over Sara was purging, getting rid of everything that no longer fit. She made piles; toss, give to the kids or grandkids, donate and keep. She found treasures as she cleaned; earrings which she promptly put on, a scarf which she folded and put in a dresser drawer but not before reminiscing about where she had gotten it and where she had last worn it. She repeated this scene again and again. The 'keep' pile was full of things Sara hadn't seen or used in years, like the key to the front door which she tucked into her purse. As the neighborhood was changing and she no longer recognized many of the men standing on Sacramento Street (Ben was no longer among them), she felt she might actually use the front door key.

Sara knew she was quite good at assessing and accepting the real, the here and now. Although she often looked back at the past with respect and reverence, she was adept at understanding where she fit into the current situation. The current situation is Leona gone, her mother, Mary, and the others having moved out of the neighborhood and out of her daily round. She acknowledged it was up to her to create a new norm.

Sara decided she needed to touch base with one of her touchstones, the one who had known and loved Sara the longest, her mother. On a whim Sara gathered up her daughters and two family friends, a car load of passengers to make a weekend trip down to Los Angeles, leaving that evening after work. The drive was uneventful, filled with chatter about Mrs. Crawford's days on Julia Street and plans for the weekend. It was an easy drive until they reached the Grapevine, known for its hilly twists and turns. Pulled to the shoulder was a long line of overheated disabled cars, owners outside trying to figure out what to do. Collectively Sara and her passengers breathed a sigh of relief when they passed through the area without incident.

Mrs. Crawford's building, a stately two story Victorian, housed four apartments, hers a studio on the second floor. When she opened the door in response to their knock Mrs. Crawford held each of them close, her embrace with Sara the longest, each taking time to 'remember' the other.

The quarters were cramped, overcrowded, hot, and they couldn't have been happier to be there. As usual Mrs. Crawford had prepared food, lots of it, and out of consideration for her guests she had done all of the frying before they arrived, to cut down on the heat. She had prepared a mountain of fried chicken, a bucket of potato salad, and an even bigger bucket of greens. And she had made her famous cornbread and pound cake. There was enough of everything to last throughout the visit. Sleeping and showering arrangements were discussed and they fell fast asleep laughing and catching up.

Early the next morning, the blistering hot sun shining directly into the studio, woke them before they were ready. It was pointless trying to sleep, the heat made it impossible. Each one got up, got dressed and had a bite to eat while a few joined Mrs. Crawford on her daily walk to the neighborhood grocery store and to her bookie. Back at the apartment plans were being made; there were many relatives in the area to visit.

First on their agenda was a trip to Sara's Aunt Ora Lee and Uncle Coy's home. It was only a few minutes away from Mrs. Crawford's studio apartment on a lovely tree-lined street. Their home boasted a wrap-around porch complete with two comfy rockers poised to ease the stress of anyone's day. The inside of the home was efficient and beautiful with homey touches everywhere the eye could see. At the back of the small space was a generous kitchen which opened onto the beautiful flower-filled backyard where all the action happened. As usual, Ora Lee was happy to see everyone, especially her niece Sara, and Coy was happy that Ora Lee was happy.

As always, whenever Sara saw her mother Tessa and her aunt Ora Lee together she was struck by the contrast between them. It was also clear that they were two sides of the same coin. The two sisters laugh at the same things; Ora Lee laughing loud and long while Tessa softly chuckles. Whenever the conversation takes a serious turn, they are saddened by the same things, pensive and thoughtful at the same times. Whenever one or the other says "remember when" Sara watched them grow young right before her eyes, as though they were girls again with Ora Lee the ringleader, planning things that were just on the edge of appropriate and Tessa gladly going along with her plans. A joy for Sara to behold.

Next on tap for the day a visit with Aunt Louella and Cousin Millie. The street they live on is grand. Though not a busy thoroughfare, the road is wide and welcoming adding to an unhurried, tranquil feel. Their single story center-hall style home is seated beautifully on an expansive lawn with mature trees on either side of the substantial walkway which leads to an extra wide but short staircase.

At the top of the stairs a gorgeous mahogany door with a brass doorknocker stands guard at the entrance. After knocking, the clack clack clack of Cousin Millie's high heels on the hard wood floor announces her arrival. When she opened the door her guests were greeted first by the faint scent of her perfume, a scent she'd worn for as long as Sara could remember. Briefly drawn to the past Sara acknowledges that scent has a memory of its own, conjuring up people and places when you least expected them. Millie is magnificent; when Ronald was a little boy he declared her "the most beautiful woman he ever saw who wasn't in a movie." Added to that she is kind and intelligent. A trifecta.

Together Aunt Louella and Cousin Millie are rather sedate (certainly compared to Ora Lee) but not at all stuffy; they are quite demonstrative when showing how happy they are to see everyone. The inside of their home is as one would expect by looking at the outside. High ceilings, crown molding, chair rails, windows encased in dark wood to match the hardwood floors and furnishings in keeping with the style of the home and its inhabitants. Moving through the hallway Aunt Louella suggested they have a seat in the living room for tea.

As Cousin Millie served the tea she inquired in general "What's new?"

Sara shared her sad news about Leona. She talked about her Statistics misadventures and eventual success and her plans for her upcoming graduation, issuing a blanket invitation. She even showed them snapshots of her afro.

"It's nice but I think this style suits you," said Aunt Louella.

By the time everyone had shared their news, Cousin Millie had gently moved the group into the dining room where the table was perfectly set and a delightful meal was served. There was ham, green beans and baby potatoes, green salad, corn bread and for desert coffee and coconut cake. The leftovers were neatly packaged and sent home with Sara. There were hugs all around and a promise from

Cousin Millie that the next time they saw her would be on Julia Street. Sara said she would hold her to her promise.

It was an easy drive back to Mrs. Crawford's home where they ate some more, talked some more until finally Mrs. Crawford declared "Now we know everything. We have an early day tomorrow so it's time we got some sleep."

Early the next morning Sara and her mother decided the two of them would walk to Mrs. Crawford's bookie. They walked arm in arm to and from the inconspicuous office in the inconspicuous building not passing more than a few words between them. On the way back, after about a block Sara said softly "One of my professors suggested I apply to Graduate School. I think I will, I think I can do it."

Squeezing her hand, her mother replied just above a whisper "I know you can."

The uneventful ride back home lulled Sara's passengers to sleep. As the others napped Sara thought of the weekend, attempting to hold on to the good feelings. She spent the quiet time reflecting and listening, quiet having rhythms of its own.

Half way home, unbidden, they came one by one telling their stories, singing their songs. Mary, Eva, Leona, even Millicent. The songs and stories were as varied as the women who had been sharing them-- staccato and brash, melodic and fleeting, sweet and low, loud and long.

"I've been the way I am all my life, it fits me. It's only a problem when people try to place their values on top of mine, making judgments based on their assumptions. There are so many ways to be. Why won't folks just let me be? By the way I separate myself from the group before I can be excluded."

"We let our insecurities get the better of us. Insecurity is insidious and it's based on assumptions. Rather than believing what we instinctively know to be true, we question and second-guess ourselves. We waste precious time talking ourselves into doing things we shouldn't and out of doing things we were born to do. I'm going to say it because I'm uniquely qualified to speak on it-- life is short. If you have the vaguest notion that you would be good at or enjoy doing something, give it a try. Believe me; failing is not the worst thing that can happen to you."

"Life is not linear, with that in mind my goal is to meet people wherever they are. Whenever I can I trumpet their strengths while quietly helping them get wherever their potential leads them."

"Just because they don't dig your brand of beauty doesn't mean you aren't beautiful."

Their voices had come to Sara clearly, convincing her that she would always remember every note.

###

Sara dropped off the last of her passengers, drove down Sacramento Street, turned right onto Julia and pulled into her driveway. For as long as she had lived in her house she had always been glad to get home. Parking the car, making her way up the stairs to the front door she found the reclaimed front door key in her handbag.

As she opened the door Sara held onto the peace she had felt all weekend surrounded by women she loved. The still of the house enveloped her as walked through the living room, down the short hallway into her bedroom to put her bag away. In the kitchen as if by rote, she made a pot of coffee and when it was done she took her place on the sofa in the living room under the window. Sara didn't turn on her music, instead she replayed the events of the weekend including the ride home.

It was the time of day that could have been daybreak or dusk, only your hold on reality confirmed one or the other. Though all alone sipping her coffee, Sara felt as if she were in a room filled with women heartened by the words they had so generously shared.

Sara didn't wait to call her mother signaling her safe arrival and to share the details of her ride home.

"Mama, we're home. No, no trouble on the road. Everybody slept until I dropped them off."

Sara wasted no time and spared no details when explaining her experience during the ride home.

"Before today I was troubled by all the 'leaving', Leona, Mary, Eva and the others." Mrs. Crawford listened intently, asking questions and making comments letting

Sara know she fully understood her experience and how she felt as a result of it.

As if to complete the experience Mrs. Crawford told her story, singing her own song. "Life is a puzzle but it doesn't come in a box with a picture on the front showing what it will look like when it's done. It's intricate, complex, colorful and the pieces fit together in unexpected ways when it's least expected."

She continued, "At first our time and energy is spent putting the perimeter of our puzzle together; setting our boundaries, creating our foundation. At the time it seems tedious and it feels as if we will never find all the pieces as they can lack color and all look the same."

"Sara", she said in earnest, "Everything in your life so far--finding a mate, having children, moving to California, starting a career have all created context, helped you create your boundaries and build your foundation. The good news is the most challenging pieces of your puzzle are now in place. From now on your pursuits; parenting your adult children, being a grandmother, continuing your schooling, nurturing your friendships and completing this phase of your career are where the magic happens. Your puzzle will become more colorful, nuanced, layered, and far less complicated.

"It won't be all smooth sailing because life, like a petulant child, will come along and knock your puzzle down, pieces will be scattered everywhere. But now it's easier to put back together because you've done it before and you know you can do it."

Sara and her mother chatted a few minutes more when Mrs. Crawford said softly "Now you know everything."

CPSIA information can be obtained
at www.ICGtesting.com
Printed in the USA
FSOW02n0132021116
26882FS